A BANTAM PATHFINDER EDITION

BANTAM PATHFINDER EDITIONS

Bantam Pathfinder Editions provide the best in
fiction and nonfiction in a wide variety of
subject areas. They include novels by classic
and contemporary writers; vivid, accurate
histories and biographies; authoritative works
in the sciences; collections of short
stories, plays and poetry.

Bantam Pathfinder Editions are carefully
selected and approved. They are durably bound,
printed on specially selected high-quality paper,
and presented in a new and handsome format.

Ellen L. Horton
P.O. Box 371
Wellton, Arizona
85356

THE MOUSE ON THE MOON

BY LEONARD WIBBERLEY

BANTAM BOOKS

BANTAM PATHFINDER EDITIONS
TORONTO / NEW YORK / LONDON

RLI: $\dfrac{\text{VLM 6.0}}{\text{IL 7.12}}$

THE MOUSE ON THE MOON
*A Bantam Book / published by arrangement with
William Morrow & Company, Inc.*

PRINTING HISTORY
Morrow edition published October 1962
2nd printing .... November 1962
3rd printing ..... February 1963
Omnibook Syndicate abridgment August and September 1963

Bantam edition published July 1963
2nd printing ...... August 1963
3rd printing ... September 1963
Bantam Pathfinder edition published February 1965
5th printing ... September 1965

6th printing

7th printing

8th printing

PRINTED IN THE UNITED STATES OF AMERICA

I

His Excellency the Count of Mountjoy, Prime Minister of the Duchy of Grand Fenwick, the world's smallest sovereign nation, located on the northern slopes of the Alps between Switzerland and France, was preparing his annual budget speech which was to be given to a meeting of the Council of Freemen, the parliament of the Duchy, on the following week.

He had before him the figures which were to be incorporated in his budget and they irritated him. He came of a long line of prime ministers, ambassadors and regents. He was of that unique breed of European (almost gone in our days) whose families have, through the centuries, provided their countries with their principal servants. And previous Counts of Mountjoy—the title dated back to the founding of the Duchy in the early part of the fifteenth century—had made notable contributions to the history of their times. Words which they had uttered at periods of crisis were still repeated with respect in the chancellories of Europe. Perhaps the most noted of such sayings was the consolation offered by the then Count to Napoleon Bonaparte after the latter's defeat at Waterloo. Coming upon the disconsolate emperor shortly after the battle, he said, "Cheer up, Sire. You can't win 'em all." The utter collapse of the Emperor and the crushing of the morale of the Imperial Armies of France has often been attributed to his remark.

For such a man, descendant as stated of a long line of august statesmen, it was galling to be dealing with a budget whose total figures could be expressed in the round in twenty thousand pounds. The breakdown of the figures was painful in the extreme, though the various headings had a most impressive ring to them.

"Allocated to the Armed Forces for the Defense of the Nation and Continuance of the Independence of its People." That was one heading, and the Count fancied it would sound well when he gave it forth to the attentive parliament. But the sum which followed—one hundred and twenty-two pounds, eighteen shillings and sixpence, three farthings—completely spoiled the effect. And the breakdown of this was indeed pathetic—thirteen pounds, two shillings and sixpence for new bowstrings; seven pounds, eighteen shillings and sixpence for

English goosefeathers with which to fletch arrows (the army of Grand Fenwick had relied through the centuries on the longbow as its principal weapon); four pounds, nine shillings and sixpence, halfpenny for bow grips. And so on.

"Bah!" cried the Count of Mountjoy as he went over these details. "What frightful and malevolent fate has condemned a man of my scope of mind to these pettifogging details, while men scarcely the master of two lines of Homer, and whose ancestors faced no problem greater than the handling of a shovel, deal in budgets involving billions."

He turned to the next item on the budget with the brave heading, "Development of Internal Communications." Oh, it sounded well enough but it consisted of an expenditure of thirty-one pounds, fifteen shillings for the repair of twelve miles of roadway (all the same road in fact) that wound through the Duchy. The Count of Mountjoy had, in vain, in previous years pleaded that this portion of the budget be greatly enlarged (it was about the same every year, as were all the other items) to permit of a bold plan for straightening parts of the road in places where it wound around the mountainsides. But nobody would listen to him. The Grand Fenwickians liked their roads narrow, winding and dangerous to a degree, although since there were no cars in the Duchy and the fastest method of travel was by bicycle, the danger was not extreme.

"A modern road program, straightening out the more tortuous sections by the construction of bridges and cuttings wherever required," the Count had argued, "would provide a considerable increase in through-traffic between France and Switzerland, with resulting revenue to ourselves."

"Fill the graveyards," said David Bentner, the solid phlegmatic leader of the Opposition. Representing the working-man of Grand Fenwick, David Bentner had a curious resort to cryptic sentences of this sort in debate, the meaning of which, he intimated, was fully understood by workingmen like himself, but utterly lost on aristocrats like the Count of Mountjoy who, never having worked with their hands, were thereby out of touch with all common sense.

"A good motor road, linking Switzerland and France, and passing through our borders could not fail to bring a most beneficial increase in tourists to our country," Mountjoy had continued.

"Fill the graveyards," said Mr. Bentner, faithful as an echo.

"We are practically the only country in Europe which is unvisited by tourists, winter or summer, and all because of our lack of facilities, for those which we have to offer can be described in one word—medieval," continued the Count.

"Fill the graveyards," said Mr. Bentner, solemn as a bell.

"If the Leader of Her Grace's Loyal Opposition would kindly stop reiterating 'Fill the graveyards' and explain what he means by that curious expression, perhaps we can continue with this debate," said Mountjoy, quite exasperated.

"Four cars passed through Grand Fenwick last year," said Mr. Bentner rising. "There were six geese killed, five ducks, four sheep dropped their lambs early and the ewes died and Ted Painter's mother has had a ringing noise in her ears ever since, as everybody knows."

"Ted Painter's mother," cried the exasperated Count of Mountjoy, "is eighty-seven years of age, as everybody also knows."

"Wonderful hearing she had until them cars went through," said Mr. Bentner. "On behalf of the working people of this country I will serve notice here and now that I would vote a flat and unyielding 'No' to any plans for making Grand Fenwick a kind of a freeway for French motor cars headed south and Swiss motor cars headed north. Besides which, you can't trust the French." Having said this, he sat down to a vigorous round of applause from his supporters, the sentiment "You can't trust the French" being well known in Grand Fenwick, which had been at war with France as late as 1475.

Mr. Bentner, representing, as has been noted, the workingmen of Grand Fenwick, was by the curious alchemy of politics a radical conservative. Although the word "conservative" to him was an expression close to poisonous, and although he regarded himself as a progressive socialist, the fact was that in the interests of the workingman, he opposed all change in the Duchy. In any change at all he saw a plot to deprive the people of work, or raise prices beyond their means, or make them produce more for the same pay; and the Count of Mountjoy had more than once remarked that his rival's political slogan should be, "Backwards With Bentner."

Mountjoy, on the other hand, was regarded by Bentner as an irresponsible dreamer who had to be watched closely lest he ruin the Duchy with schemes which would appall a nation as daring in economical matters as the United States of America. The one was the perfect counterweight to the other, and between the two of them, the Duchy of Grand Fenwick, a sovereign nation of fifteen square miles, but of remarkable world prestige, ambled along through the fearful decades of the twentieth century.

The prestige of the Duchy of Grand Fenwick came (as

has been related elsewhere) * from its defeat of the United States of America when, desperate for money, it had conceived the plan of declaring war on that nation. It was argued, history providing an excellent precedent, that if the Duchy declared war on the United States on Monday, it would be defeated by Tuesday and a glorious rehabilitation of the nation as a defeated enemy would certainly be under way by Friday night. But the plan had gone awry. Tully Bascomb, in charge of the handful of longbowmen sent to invade New York, had fumbled the whole thing and with the capture of a weapon of mass destruction called the Q-bomb, together with its inventor, Dr. Kokintz, won, rather than lost, the war.

The bomb now rested in the Duchy, representing, together with two hundred longbows, several suits of mail and the necessary arrows, the complete and astonishing armament of the country. Possessed of the bomb, Grand Fenwick had formed a League of Little Nations with the smaller countries of the world, and had been able to enforce an atomic inspection of the other nations. An uneasy peace between East and West ensued. But the inspection, the result of coercion rather than sincere agreement, was not working. Atomic rearmament was going on in spite of it. The bigger nations grew bigger and more menacing. The smaller nations dwindled to insignificance. The rivalry for control of the earth was even being taken into space, so that mastery of the moon and the planets was now part of the ambitions of East and West.

It was not surprising then that it maddened the Count of Mountjoy, coming as he did of such distinguished diplomatic lineage, that he should be concerned with a budget of less than twenty thousand pounds while his counterparts in other nations juggled with billions and calculated the orbit to the moon and East vied with West for the mastery of space. The Count had an active and imaginative mind which operated on the grand scale. But as Prime Minister of so small a nation, his scope was tremendously reduced and all the plans which he could evolve within the scope allotted to him were frustrated, year after year, by the arch conservatism of the Opposition led by Mr. Bentner.

These plans included not only the straightening of the twelve miles of road through the Duchy to encourage tourism. Even dearer to the Count's heart was the modernization of the plumbing in the castle of Grand Fenwick, in which he had his apartments. He had fought for this project for fifteen years and got nowhere. Such plumbing as the castle had was in a word barbarous. The Count was compelled to wash in

* *The Mouse That Roared.*

water brought to his chambers in a ewer, for when the castle was built at the close of the thirteenth century, no piping had been put through the walls.

The water was obtained from a well in the courtyard and then heated in a caldron over the kitchen fires. By the time it came to him up three hundred steps of a circular staircase, it was invariably tepid if not downright cold. The services of two men and a boy were required to get sufficient water heated and rushed to the Count's apartments so that he might bathe in a hip bath which was two hundred years old and leaked dismally from some unlocatable hole along its seam.

What applied to the Count, of course, applied to Her Grace the Duchess Gloriana XII, ruler of Grand Fenwick, and her consort, Tully Bascomb, and all the other occupants of the castle. But try as he might, the Count could never get the Council of Freemen to vote sufficient funds to install modern plumbing, or agree to borrowing the money from the United States, which he was sure would certainly sanction the loan.

Angered at the impossibility of obtaining from the obdurate Bentner so small a convenience as hot and cold water throughout the castle, the Count pushed the budget material aside on his desk and went off to see Dr. Kokintz, the eminent developer of the Q-bomb, now alas an almost archaic weapon with the possibility of a neutron bomb in sight.

He found Dr. Kokintz in his study in the castle, seated before an excellent fire and deeply immersed in a book on birds, for he was devoted to ornithology and his study was gay with cages of birds which he cared for himself and all of which he called by name.

"Ah, good evening, Mountjoy," Kokintz said when the Count entered. "I have just had the most exciting news from Bascomb."

"Oh?" said Mountjoy.

"Yes. Two bobolinks have been found in the forest. Bascomb did not see them closely but he believes they are male and female. Just think of it. There have been no bobolinks in Grand Fenwick in all its history. Now these two little visitors come to us and perhaps will make their home in our forest. I am going down to the forest tomorrow with Bascomb, and we are going to spend the whole day trying to get a picture of them. I can assure you that the Audubon Society will be very interested. In fact astounded. But as you know there is a shrike about, in the southern edge of the forest, and his presence is very serious indeed."

"A shrike?" asked Mountjoy.

"Yes. A butcher bird. They are demons among birds, nip-

ping the heads off their fellow creatures and devouring them.
It would be appalling if the shrike were to discover the
bobolinks and perhaps kill one or the other of them. We
may have to kill the shrike. Bascomb says it can be done,
though it may take a day or two. He says unfortunately
there are no funds in his budget for this kind of work. Do
you think something could be managed when you make
your budget speech next week? The bobolinks are very important."

Mountjoy groaned aloud. Bobolinks and shrikes. These
were the problems placed before such a man as he.

"Yes," he said savagely, "I expect Bentner will permit the
expenditure of a few shillings to protect two bobolinks. But
I was hoping for conversation of a somewhat larger scope
when I came to see you."

"Ah," said Kokintz, "you have no feeling for birds. It is a
pity. They are so cheerful and bright at all times. Indeed,
of all creatures birds are the busiest and gayest. And in times
such as these, my friend, we need their company."

The scientist rose and, going to a cupboard, brought forth
a bottle of Pinot Grand Fenwick, that noble wine for which
(perhaps even more than its defeat of the United States of
America) the Duchy was famed throughout the civilized
world.

He placed two glasses on a small table before the fire,
fumbled in his pocket and took out an old-fashioned clasp-
knife he had had since he was a boy. The knife was almost
a museum piece, containing not only several blades but also
an implement for the removal of stones from horses' hoofs,
a gimlet, a screw driver, a can opener and a corkscrew.

Kokintz opened the corkscrew and while Mountjoy shiv-
ered in agony that so great a wine should be tapped by so
ignoble an instrument, drew the cork. Then he carefully
poured a glass of the Pinot for himself and another for
Mountjoy, and then with a slight salute, and again to the
horror of the Count, drained his glass in one swallow.

"That," said Mountjoy, "is Premier Grand Cru 'Fifty-eight
—the greatest Pinot we have produced in fifty years."

"Very good too," said Kokintz, on whom this rebuke was
utterly lost. He poured himself another glass and then taking
an apple out of his pocket, cut a piece from it with his clasp
knife and put the piece in the bars of a cage containing two
black and white rice birds.

"They like a piece of apple now and again, but too much
is bad for them." He beamed as the rice birds pecked away
at the apple, fluttering with ecstasy.

"Who do you think will be first in the moon?" asked

Mountjoy desperate to head the conversation in a direction worthy of his mentality.

"A monkey," said Kokintz. "You remember our little childhood saying? Well, first man on the moon is a monkey." He chuckled at the thought. "A monkey and maybe a mouse. After that—a man. If, of course, the monkey survives and can be brought back."

"Do you think it will be a Russian monkey or an American monkey?" asked Mountjoy.

"African, most likely," said Kokintz. "They are hardier. And small."

"But will it be a Russian rocket that takes it there or an American rocket?"

Kokintz shrugged. "Who am I to say?" he asked. "I read what I can here. But it is what one cannot read that is important. I would say, however, that the Russians are likely to succeed first. They have already put a rocket on the moon. They have already orbited an astronaut several times around the earth; so has the United States, but the Russians were first. They are probably ahead in the only remaining problem, which is that of getting a rocket back from the moon.

"That is a really difficult problem. The earth's gravity, which as you know is several times greater than that of the moon, will accelerate the speed of a rocket approaching earth tremendously. And the increasing density of the atmosphere around the earth would produce such a terrible friction that the rocket is likely to burn up like a meteor.

"Of course there are ways of combating these difficulties which are well known to physicists. But I would suspect that the Russians are further ahead with the actual work and are therefore likely to succeed before the United States of America."

"What is the major problem involved in getting a rocket to the moon?" asked Mountjoy, whose thoughts recently had been much occupied with the space race.

"Energy," replied Kokintz, seating himself again by the fire. "Fuel. The discovery of a source of energy sufficiently powerful to project the rocket from the earth to the moon. Present fuels are oxygen-activated—that is to say, they burn oxygen to release their energy. Some of them are liquid, some solid with built-in oxygen, for as you realize there is no oxygen available in space. But none of these fuels is much more than primitive. An entirely new energy source is required for space travel."

They fell silent for a while, Mountjoy envying those nations whose budgets could command research into so fascinating a problem and Kokintz engaged with the whole field of energy, of which man knew so little.

What was energy? It was a form of matter. All matter could be converted into energy if the key for the conversion could be found. And the corollary of that statement was that all energy could be converted into matter—an even more fascinating prospect. Nothing was ever destroyed and all things were therefore eternal though they changed their forms. He found the thought greatly comforting.

His mind wandered off into this infinity of the interrelationship of energy and matter and the Count of Mountjoy, seeing him thus preoccupied, left the room disconsolate, to return to the petty problem of the budget of Grand Fenwick.

When he had gone, Kokintz continued staring at the low heavy oak table before him as if upon its top lay the whole universe and all its mysteries. He was a pudgy man in his late sixties with a figure that would have done credit to a teddy bear. One of the world's greatest physicists, he was essentially a simple man and his colleagues agreed that it was his basic simplicity which made him so great a scientist. He had an ability to see clearly through the most complicated issues, never distracted by fascinating pitfalls to the side.

He did most of his work with paper and pencil, and since it irritated him to be without a pencil when he needed one, he carried a dozen or more on his person, so that the breastpocket of his jacket bulged with pencils of many kinds. Tully Bascomb had once counted the number of pencils Dr. Kokintz had about his person and found seventeen. When Dr. Kokintz wanted to test any calculation he had conjured up, he sent the ingredients off to the Institute for Advanced Studies at Princeton, or to the California Institute of Technology or some such institution, and these were always glad to do whatever he required.

So he sat, staring at the table top, when suddenly there was a little pop and the cork flipped out of the bottle of Pinot on the table before him. Kokintz stared at the bottle and the cork and then looked from them to the fire.

"Boyle's law of the expansion of gases," he said to himself. And then, because such was his type of mind, he began to wonder exactly what rise in temperature had taken place inside the bottle to cause the fumes from the wine to become sufficiently agitated to push the cork out of the bottle. Was it the same for all wines? Certainly not. That would depend on their volatility, which was related to their alcoholic content. But was there something about Pinot Grand Fenwick, a wine prized throughout the world for its bouquet and its health-giving qualities? . . .

Dr. Kokintz picked up the bottle and then did something that would have horrified the Count of Mountjoy. He measured a portion of the Premier Grand Cru '58 into a beaker and then poured it into a retort, and fumbling around for a match—he was a pipe smoker and never had any—found one at last and lit a Bunsen burner under the retort.

He became so interested in what he was doing that he was still at his work, his desk littered with books and technical reports from scientists in every corner of the globe, when the following day dawned.

II

Dr. Kokintz was extremely tired, having had no sleep at all when Tully Bascomb called on him the following morning so that they could get pictures of the bobolinks for their report to the Audubon Society.

Tully was politically the most important man in the Duchy of Grand Fenwick, being the consort of the regnant Duchess, Gloriana XII, a somewhat willful young lady of twenty-three. His relationship to her was that of Prince Albert to the great English queen, Victoria. He was at one and the same time her adviser, her investigator and her conscience in so far as it was concerned with the affairs of the Duchy. But he held her in the greatest reverence and made no effort himself to become the ruler of Grand Fenwick or to detract from the regard in which she was held by her people. His own devotion to Gloriana, who was both his wife and his ruler, was a magnificent example to the five thousand seven hundred and sixty-three inhabitants of Grand Fenwick, whose loyalty and love for the pretty Duchess had indeed deepened since her marriage to Tully Bascomb.

Besides his position as Ducal Consort, Tully was also (by virtue of his own talents) Grand Marshal of the Duchy, meaning, in modern terms, Commander-in-Chief of the Armed Forces, and also Chief Steward (which in modern terms would be the equivalent of Secretary of the Interior). It will be understood that the various government posts in Grand Fenwick still retained their medieval titles. As Chief Steward his duties included supervision of the Forest of Grand Fenwick—an area of no more than three hundred acres lying at the bottom of the valley whose mountainous walls marked the boundaries of the country. He had traveled much in his youth but was fond of forestry and together with

Dr. Kokintz, had contrived to turn the Forest of Grand Fenwick into a sanctuary for wild life.

"Been working?" asked Tully, glancing around the disorderly office and sniffing the air, in which there was a strong smell of wine.

"Ah yes," said Kokintz, rubbing his eyes. "Yes. A little work. The chemistry of wine has been curiously neglected. Some research has been done here and there but no real digging. Now what did I do with that residue?" He went over to his work bench and its litter of books, pipettes, retorts and beakers and peered around clucking impatiently to himself. Then he started patting his pockets and took out of them a large Oompaul pipe and then the apple of which he had given a piece to the rice birds. The apple had gone brown in the area which was cut and he examined this brown color with interest and for a moment seemed to have forgotten the object of his search.

"The residue," said Tully gently.

"Huh?" said Kokintz. "Ah yes. The residue." He gave one more look at the apple and then took a huge bite out of it to provide his breakfast. He put the remainder back in his pocket and started opening and shutting the books which were lying around, sometimes stopping to read a paragraph which caught his eye.

"Tanashi of Tokyo," he said, tapping the pages of one book. "A sound man. He has done a great deal of work on the effect of spatial radiation on the growth of bamboos and other giant grasses." He turned to another book, grunted, picked up a yellowed sheet of printed paper and grunted again. "Potato virus." And was lost for a while in reading.

"The residue," said Tully gently.

"What residue?" said Dr. Kokintz.

"Whatever residue you were looking for," said Tully.

"Of course. Of course," said Kokintz and turned once more to his haphazard search, being rewarded after a little time by the discovery of an envelope into which he peered mildly and then, folding it up, put in his pocket.

He turned to Tully. "What have you got that camera for?" he asked.

"We are going to get pictures of the bobolinks," said Tully, who was quite accustomed to Kokintz' absent-mindedness.

"Of course," said Kokintz. "Yes. Here, let me carry those plates for you." He took a number of the photographic plates from Tully and stuffed them into the pocket of his coat and the two left together for the forest. On the way, Tully began to feel apologetic about dragging the scientist away from his work and, to ease his conscience, said if what the doctor was doing was very important, perhaps they could return on the following day and get the pictures of the bobolinks. Or alternately, he could try to get them himself.

"Oh no," said Kokintz. "It is no great matter. It is just a little research." He offered nothing further, and they trudged along in silence until they came to the border of the forest, which was ringed about by a fence of rails. They climbed the fence and, pushing through the tangle of last year's bracken, for the month was March, came at last to the area in which the bobolinks had been seen. Here they constructed a shelter of brushwood for their camera, which was focused on the topmost branches of a beech tree in which the birds had been spotted the previous day. They waited through the forenoon and the greater part of the afternoon and were rewarded with twelve exposures, of which three promised to be excellent, being taken through a telescopic lens.

During this waiting Kokintz took out one of the innumerable pencils which he always carried in the breastpocket of his coat and made a great quantity of calculations on a large block of paper which he had brought with him.

He fell asleep shortly after midday and Tully, glancing at the pages on which the doctor had made his calculations, was surprised to find a picture of a bottle of wine on one of them. Nearby was scrawled "Temp. 68 deg. F." and below that "Thrust 20 lbs. per square inch minimum."

None of this made much sense to him though he concluded that the doctor was busy with the problem of the fermentation of Pinot Grand Fenwick. When they had exposed all their plates they returned to the castle and Dr. Kokintz said that he would develop the negatives himself. Tully was content to let him do this, for in these matters the doctor was the most careful worker.

While Tully and Dr. Kokintz were in the Forest of Grand Fenwick, the Count of Mountjoy was making his daily call on Her Grace the Duchess Gloriana. He found the Duchess propped up in bed and leafing through one of the slick American magazines which formed her favorite reading. The magazine which occupied her attention was *Holiday* and at the sight of it the Count had a moment of misgiving. Gloriana had several times mentioned the prospect of taking a vacation abroad with her consort and the finances of the Duchy could not extend to such a trip.

"I hope you haven't decided to bore me with the budget figures, Bobo," said Gloriana, eying the Count severely. "I'm not in a mood to talk about it now, and in any case you know I like to have Tully with me whenever money has to be discussed."

"No, Your Grace," said the Count meekly.

"Well, sit down then and have a little toast," said Gloriana. "The marmalade is over there but there's only one knife and that's got butter on it. Still, I don't mind if you get butter in the marmalade."

The Count smiled and helped himself to toast and marmalade. He was much older than the Duchess, old enough in fact to be her father and that by a handsome margin. As a baby she could never pronounce his name, Mountjoy, and called him Bobo instead and that was the name she used except when she was very angry with him.

"Your Grace was thinking of going on a vacation?" asked the Count, eying the magazine meaningly.

"No," said Gloriana. "Not a vacation. Something better than a vacation—for a woman, at least."

"Oh?" said the Count, cautiously.

"Bobo, would you help me to get something that I really need desperately? I just have to have it." Her voice and manner had all the direct and disarming simplicity of a child's. It was the tone of voice that Gloriana had used on him with success ever since she was five years of age, and Mountjoy knew that he was helpless in the face of it. He tried to temporize.

"I must know what it is before I can promise," he said.

"That isn't very gallant," said Gloriana. "It isn't what I expect of you. You used to be always willing to do what I wanted. Now you're getting old and cagey."

"I am still Your Grace's devoted servant," said Mountjoy, "though I admit to the weight of years."

"Now you're trying to be pathetic," said Gloriana. "But it won't work. Tell me, how can you pretend to be my devoted servant when you won't promise to get me what I want without knowing what it is first? What's devoted about that? If you're devoted, you don't bargain with people. You just do what they ask."

Mountjoy knew he was beaten and was mildly surprised that he had, in view of his past experience, nurtured even the faintest hope that the outcome would be different.

"I promise, Your Grace," he said. "Whatever it is you want, I will use my best endeavors to get it for you."

"Bobo, you're a darling," said Gloriana. "And I didn't mean that about getting cagey and old. You are the only man who really understands women. Absolutely the only one. Tully doesn't at all."

"Thank you, Your Grace," said the Count of Mountjoy. "What is it that Your Grace desires?"

"A fur coat," said Gloriana.

"A fur coat?" cried Mountjoy, astonished.

"Yes," said Gloriana. "An Imperial Russian Sable coat. They're absolutely divine. One of those. Just look at it. Isn't it heavenly?"

She threw the copy of *Holiday* to the Count of Mountjoy and he picked it up to examine a picture of a woman swathed luxuriously in an Imperial Russian Sable fur coat. Clad in the rich, deep black fur, the woman looked like an empress and for a moment the Count of Mountjoy recalled with nostalgia the great days in Europe before World War I when women attended the opera at Covent Garden or in Paris clad in just such furs, and men wore top hats and cloaks lined in white or red silk, and talked of grouse shooting in Scotland or pig-sticking in India and discussed the coq au vin on the *Lusitania* or the qualities of Belgian guns for tiger shooting. Looking at that fur, a whole world, which had been a wonderful world for his kind, reappeared before him.

But the cost—the cost was impossible. It was around fifty thousand dollars, sixteen or seventeen thousand pounds; the equivalent, in fact, of the total budget of Grand Fenwick for a full year. He paled at the thought of the expense and was dismayed that he had been trapped into promising to use his best endeavors to satisfy this desire of the Duchess. Gloriana noted his reaction and said airily, "Is something the matter, Bobo?"

"It's the expense, Your Grace," said the Count. "I do not know how or where we are to get the money. It is beyond our means."

Gloriana did not say anything to this immediately. Rather, she took a piece of toast, spread some marmalade on it with great nicety and then gave it to the Count, who at that particular moment had no appetite for the tidbit.

"Sometimes you underestimate your own abilities, Bobo," she said at length coaxingly. "You have dealt for so long in little things that your view of your own potentialities is reduced. You are made small by smallness, but you are a man who is capable of greatness. I am surprised to see you dismayed at the prospect of getting me a fur coat."

The Count felt a little swelling of confidence at these words, and at the same time was ashamed at his dismay over the cost of the coat. But there rose before him the picture of Bentner with his opposition to expenditures of any kind, particularly expenditures which involved borrowing money.

And certainly if the Duchess was to be provided with a fur coat, the money would have to be borrowed.

"We are a nation," Gloriana said firmly. "We are a small nation but a real nation, just like all the other nations of the world. A private person might be appalled at the thought of the cost of such a purchase. But it is utterly ridiculous to think that a nation—any nation—cannot provide its ruler with a fur coat."

"It *is* ridiculous," agreed the Count. "But it is also true."

"It is only true if you admit that it is true," said Gloriana firmly. "I have already warned you against underestimating yourself and being dragged down by the little things you have to deal with. You haven't been able to get hot and cold water for us nor a good road through the Duchy but I certainly think you ought to be able to get me a fur coat and I'm going to leave the problem up to you. I'm the only ruler in Europe that has to go around in a cloth coat and even if it is of the best Irish handwoven tweed, it isn't fair."

With that she closed the audience, and the Count of Mountjoy, put on his mettle by the Duchess, whom he loved, went away to do some very hard thinking—alone.

III

The Count of Mountjoy did nobly in the presentation of his budget to the Council of Freemen with which, as usual, he coupled a review of international affairs. Even the stolid David Bentner had to admit that on this occasion the Count had excelled himself. His summary of international affairs was masterly, his picture of the Iron Curtain being extended into space ("affrighting the silence of the spheres with the strident nationalism of man" was the way the Count put it) drew shivers of appreciation even from the Labor back bench. His solemn warning that in times such as these there was a grave charge upon Grand Fenwick to lead East and West into the ways of sanity brought resounding cheers from both sides of the House, since no real effort or cash expenditure was involved.

"In such times as these," the Count continued, "when all the resources of human wisdom are needed to ensure the future happiness of mankind and his security on his mother planet, it behooves us to be cautious in all matters and to guard well all expenditures undertaken by the nation. The opposition will, I think, be pleased to hear that I have therefore included in the budget no provision whatever for extraordinary expenses such as the improvement of communications within the Duchy or the installation of modern plumbing in the castle, which I have so often advocated, though without success in the past." (Cautious cheers from the Opposition, which scented a trap in these concessions.)

"However," continued the Count, "I ask both sides of the House to support me in an application for special credits from the United States . . ."

"No loans . . . no loans . . ." shouted Bentner.

"An application for special credits from the United States . . ."

"No loans . . ." cried Bentner. "Who borrows money sells himself."

". . . for the purpose of . . ."

Bentner was about to interrupt again when he was gaveled into silence by the Speaker.

". . . for the purpose," continued the Count, "of gratifying a wish dear to our most gracious lady, Her Grace, the Duchess Gloriana XII, ensuring her prestige, her dignity, and that of her people."

Bentner was immediately put out of countenance. The Duchess was not present at this budget address, for the constitution forbade the ruler of Grand Fenwick taking any hand in matters concerning the raising of money—a proper provision against arbitrary tax demands. But it was traditional that whatever the ruler desired should, within reason, be granted, and any suggestion at all of opposition to such desires, particularly in the case of Gloriana, smacked of a kind of personal treason and disloyalty horrible to think upon.

"As leader of Her Grace's Loyal Opposition," said Bentner, "I ask permission to point out to the House that in my interruptions of the Prime Minister, I meant no disloyalty whatever to Her Grace."

The speaker grunted, whispered to the clerk of the House, and Mountjoy, who now had Bentner at a disadvantage, went on.

"I am going to take the unusual step of asking that for the next several minutes the House consider itself as a committee sitting *in camera*. We can resume the open debate upon the budget later. But the details I wish to produce now should be the more effective if they are kept secret from Her Grace, for the time being, though they can be released later. In short, I would like to surprise her."

The Speaker consulted with the clerk and then glanced at Bentner, who, having been discomfited once, was not going to risk being discomfited again by raising an objection. He was no great parliamentarian and was constantly outmaneuvered in this department by the Count.

"It is the sense of the House," said the Speaker, "that the open meeting upon the budget has been recessed until I summon it into session again, and the House is meeting now as a committee of the whole *in camera*." The clerk's goose quill squeaked as he recorded this in the official minute book.

"Excellent," said the Count of Mountjoy. "And now to business which I would ask you to bear in mind is secret. Her Grace has expressed the desire to obtain an Imperial Russian Sable fur coat. As members are undoubtedly aware, Imperial Russian Sables are those furs of so high a quality that their use was once limited to members of the former royal family of Russia. The cost of a coat, full length, made of such furs would be in the neighborhood of sixteen thousand pounds—fifty thousand dollars in round figures. [There was a gasp at this, but Mountjoy plunged on.] This is the equivalent of the total financial resources of the Duchy of Grand Fenwick for one year, and funds therefore cannot be provided out of our own revenue without such a monstrous increase in taxes that it is not to be contemplated."

"Hear, hear," said Bentner stoutly.

"We are faced therefore with the situation of either having to deny our Duchess this request, or of obtaining the money in the form of a loan from the United States, repayable perhaps over a period of thirty or forty years and at a low rate of interest.

"I am sure that members will agree with me that it would be a hard thing indeed if we have to go to our liege lady and tell her that this nation, over which she and her ancestors have ruled with such fidelity, love and devotion for six hundred years, cannot provide her with a fur coat. I myself have not the heart to bear her such a message, and I am sure that the members of the Opposition would themselves be unable to be the bearers of such tidings. It is not, I am sure, in the nature of the men of Grand Fenwick to deny their lady this request."

In the short silence that followed there was a murmur about the Council chamber. Mountjoy, a good parliamentarian and very sensitive to the atmosphere of the House, was well aware that he had not all the members with him. He knew that men's minds may often be operated through their hearts, and when a matter might not be carried by an appeal to reason, then an appeal to emotion was the best resource. It was time to make an emotional appeal now.

"Members may well ask themselves, though privately, whether this is not an unreasonable request of the Duchess upon her people. They may ask, and they may be forgiven for asking, whether there is not in this request some tinge of selfishness, of womanly vanity, unworthy of our sovereign lady and foreign to that sweetness and grace of character of which we have all been the beneficiaries. They may secretly inquire of themselves what services she has rendered; what sacrifices she has made, to put so heavy a request before her people.

"My friends, let me attempt to supply the answers to these questions. Our sovereign lady is a woman in the full beauty of womanhood, who never before has put any onerous burden upon her people. Indeed, rather than ask anything of them, she has freely given to them all the gifts (and they are many) which she has at her disposal. Other women, of lower station, and I would venture to say of less strength of character and intelligence, may and, indeed, have carved for themselves brilliant careers in industry, in the arts, in letters, making the purchase of a fur coat, such as Her Grace desires, something readily within their private means. These others own their lives, are responsible only to themselves, can use their abilities and their talents to promote their own careers and their own fortunes. Completely free, no country in the world is denied them, no profession or career is closed to them. Their lives are their own.

"Such is not true of Her Grace.

"Her life, from birth, has belonged to her people. All countries are closed to her, for, in duty to her people, she must remain here. All careers, all professions—all use of her talents in the arts for her own advancement and satisfaction—are denied her. Her mind, her talents, her spirit, her ambitions, her hopes—all these she gives freely to her people here in Grand Fenwick.

"My friends, she has given us, she continues to give us, her life in its entirety, freely making the loving sacrifice of sovereigns that every breath they draw belongs to their people. Are we to tell her that we cannot give her in return a fur coat?"

"No! No!" cried the whole House led by Bentner.

Mountjoy smiled, paused and looked around. "There is one other aspect of this matter to be considered," he continued. "I will call it a political matter though perhaps the better word is patriotic. You are all aware, I am sure, of the great and beneficial impression which has been made upon the world by the wardrobe and personal appearance of the gracious wife of the President of the United States. You are aware, no doubt, also of the equally good impression made upon the world by the charming appearance of England's queen, Elizabeth II. We have a right to ask ourselves whether our own Duchess should appear less elegantly attired than these. We have a right to consider whether our own Duchess, in future visits to foreign countries, can properly represent her own dignity and that of her people and realm clad in a cloth coat—though of good handwoven tweed."

"No! No!" cried Bentner. "Never."

"Precisely," said the Count of Mountjoy. "I take it then that the sentiment of the House is that I should be authorized to apply to the United States of America for funds sufficient for this purpose?"

"Right," cried Bentner, glaring around at his supporters.

"I thank you on behalf of Her Grace," said the Count of Mountjoy.

"We shall require that in the form of a motion," said the Speaker airily.

The Count of Mountjoy popped his monocle in his eye, glared himself at the Speaker, inspected the benches of the Opposition across the floor from him, and then with a twitch of his eyebrow permitted the monocle to drop, glittering like a diamond, to his waist where it swung suspended on a chain of little gold links.

"I move," he said, "that the Prime Minister of the Duchy of Grand Fenwick be given permission to apply to the Government of the United States of America for a loan of funds sufficient to ensure the continuing prestige of Her Grace and of her people."

The wording was curious but Bentner, anxious to redeem himself as a loyal and loving subject of the Duchess, promptly jumped to his feet and cried, "I second the motion."

The vote was unanimous. The decision, to present the Imperial Russian Sable coat to the Duchess on her birthday, which was the twentieth of October, and until then nothing was to be said further on the matter.

The Count of Mountjoy and Bentner left the Council chamber in unusual accord, each with the sense of having performed a good day's work.

IV

The rude winds of March stormed across the eastern seaboard of the United States, howling over the flatlands of New Jersey, hissing and shrilling around the battlements of New York and flinging all into a turbulence as far inland as the national capital.

Seated in his office in Washington D.C., the United States Secretary of State scowled at the flurries of rain and sleet that slashed against the windows opposite his desk, seeing in them a reflection of the furies at work in the world of international affairs—furies which his best efforts had failed to abate after three years in office.

He envied his predecessors of a few decades back who had, for all the troubles of their times, lived in a world with a set and established number of nations, whose histories, economic needs and political ambitions were well known to them.

How different matters were now! New nations were popping into being as fast as mushrooms under a full moon. Twenty independent nations had come into existence in Africa in one year alone—some of them the equal of, or even bigger than, some of the oldest nations in Europe. He frequently found himself called upon to advise the President on countries so new their boundaries were not marked on the latest maps, their leaders had, a year before, been unknown ten miles from their birthplace, and their economic needs, social backgrounds, religious and other conflicts were beyond the knowledge of any of his staff.

Diplomacy in dealing with such countries had been reduced to a guessing game. And at the thought the Secretary smiled grimly. For, in a sense, diplomacy had always been a guessing game. There was no other way to account for the colossal blunderings of all nations throughout their histories, in their dealings with each other. You got together all the information you could, and then you made a guess. Brilliant diplomats were actually men with a talent for guessing right and the same was true of brilliant generals and brilliant presidents.

To reduce the hazards of this guessing game, the Secretary of State insisted that all communications addressed to him from foreign governments should be brought to his attention only when accompanied by a full summary of all the pertinent facts. This summary of pertinent facts, obtained from the heads of particular "desks" in his department, was always forwarded to the Secretary of State in a Red Folder —the color of the folder indicating immediately that the information was complete.

As many as a dozen of these Red Folders were placed on the Secretary's desk during the course of a normal day. There was a pile of them before him now and after contemplating the gloomy condition of both the weather and international affairs, the Secretary picked up the first of them.

On it was a label reading "Duchy of Grand Fenwick." The Secretary frowned, experiencing a little tremor of anxiety, well aware of the trouble the United States had experienced with this little nation in the past. He felt indeed like putting the Grand Fenwick folder aside and turning to the next, which was marked "West Germany" and which, despite the still unresolved Berlin question, might prove less explosive. But the Secretary was Vermont-born and his boyhood training, which had insisted that he never turn aside from anything which was difficult or unpleasant, got the better of him. He braced himself and opened the Grand Fenwick Red Folder, and started reading the topmost paper in it.

This consisted of an official communication from the Duchy to the Government of the United States. It was written on the official stationery of the Duchy, with the ducal arms spread across the top. The seal of the Duchy, imprinted over a piece of green ribbon, was attached to the bottom with to the side of it, the signature "Mountjoy" written in an expressive hand. Below the signature was the title "Principal Minister of State to Her Grace, Gloriana XII." The document, as was the case with all communications from Grand Fenwick, was not typed but written in longhand and with a goose-quill pen. It was as neatly done as the original of the United States Declaration of Independence (the Count of Mountjoy had written it himself) and it carried with it some of the authority and indeed grandeur of that splendid document. The letter read:

The Secretary of State
Government of the United States of America
Washington, D.C.

Greetings:
I have the honor to inform you that at a meeting of the full representation of the Council of Freemen of the Duchy of Grand Fenwick, held on March the fifth, the undersigned, as Her Grace's Principal Minister of State, was authorized to apply to the Government of the United States of America for a loan-in-aid, the precise wording of the enabling resolution being: "A loan of funds sufficient to ensure the continuing prestige of Her Grace and of her people."

The amount sought to achieve this estimable purpose, which I am sure will be heartily supported by the Government of the United States (whose welfare we in the Duchy of Grand Fenwick have always close to our hearts) is $5,050,000. Of this sum $5,000,000 is required to finance a project to send a manned rocket to the moon and $50,000 is to be applied to the purchase of a fur coat for Her Grace the Duchess to surprise her on her birthday. . . .

"What the devil!" cried the Secretary of State aloud to his

empty room when he had read this. "Five million dollars to go to the moon and fifty thousand for a fur coat. I've never heard of anything more nonsensical in my life."

He flung the Red Folder down on the desk in front of him, flipped a switch on the interoffice telephone and snarled into it, "Wendover, have the goodness to come to my office this moment." He flipped the switch back without waiting for a reply. In a matter of seconds Frederick Paxton Wendover, in charge of the Central European desk of the State Department, was in the Secretary's office, cool and collected and anxious to be of help.

Frederick Paxton Wendover was known among his colleagues on the second level of the State Department hierarchy as a man to watch. They agreed that while he was hardly likely ever to become Secretary of State, being incapable of making a public utterance or of creating any warm personal impression on others, he was one of those whose knowledge and insight into foreign affairs, particularly Central European affairs, would provide sure guidance for many Secretaries less brilliant than himself.

In his personal appearance he was as close to anonymity as a human being can achieve. Nobody, even the closest of his colleagues, could give a good physical description of him. There was a certain studiousness about him, and he gave people the impression of wearing rimless glasses and wire ear pieces. Many were surprised to discover on checking on this detail that he didn't wear glasses at all. He just looked like a man who wore glasses. He was of medium size and medium weight. He always wore suits of the same pattern and color. Some thought they were of dark gray and others dark olive. Actually they were dark brown, but again nobody had ever really noticed. His hair was fair and thin, his eyebrows so slight as to be scarcely seen, and he wore a small moustache which was his one vanity. But no one had noticed when he started to grow it and indeed it was hardly discernible upon his upper lip.

The physical appearance of Wendover then lacked any cold or positive assertion. His temperament was as mild as his appearance. But his mind was better stocked in his own specialties than any other man's in the government. He had a tremendous grasp of the history and character of the Central European nations, spoke not only their various languages but dialects of their languages, knew their folklore as well as he knew their economics and was able to do that which it is so difficult for most Americans to do—think like a European while remaining an American. His loyalty to his own country was beyond question. His understanding of others beyond parallel. Even the sight of Wendover standing before him helped to quell the wrath of the Secretary of State and restored some order to his outraged mind. He beckoned him to a chair and stabbing with a finger in the direction of the offending Red Folder said, "I suppose this isn't some joke of yours?"

It was typical of Wendover that he did not reply immediately, but instead picked up the Red Folder, opened it, glanced at the letter from the Count of Mountjoy and then said, "No, sir."

"Well, what the devil is the meaning of it then?" demanded the Secretary. "I can't believe what I read. Five million dollars for a rocket and fifty thousand dollars for a fur coat? What in hell am I to make of *that?* Are *they* pulling some kind of a joke?"

"Oh no, sir," said Wendover. "Mountjoy is in earnest, I am quite sure. You didn't read the full communication? . . ." There was a suggestion of a rebuke in the question.

"No," snapped the Secretary. "I did not."

"I think it would be better if you read it through, sir," said Wendover, and the Secretary picked up the Red Folder again and with a scowl at Wendover continued with his reading.

In your approach to the Congress for the funds required [the letter continued], you will naturally require to know for what reason the Duchy of Grand Fenwick wishes to send a manned rocket to the moon.

In several recent statements, your own President has supplied the main ground for this project, urging the internationalization of the exploration of space, and stressing that it would be disastrous if the quarrels of nations on earth should be extended to proprietorship of the moon. Commendable efforts have been made by the United States, working through the United Nations, to secure agreement for international control of the moon—but without effect. It is plain that the old law of discovery, granting prior rights to the first to land, is likely to hold sway in space.

In these circumstances, Her Grace's government deems it a grave charge upon Grand Fenwick to intervene and to send a manned rocket to the moon at this point, so that a third power, representing nations other than the Big Two, is involved in the matter. This would have the effect of truly internationalizing the conquest of the moon as is the expressed desire of your President, and we are sure that the Congress will wish to implement the desire of the President by voting the necessary funds.

The fur coat. . . .

But the Secretary didn't want to read about the fur coat and putting the folder down, looked dazedly at Wendover.

"They can't be serious," he said.

"They are serious," said Wendover calmly. "That is to say, Mountjoy is serious, though I suspect that this is all a plan of his own, and that he is applying for something for which he has not got specific authorization. He is a wildly imaginative and ambitious man. He is a firm believer in personal connivance as an instrument of government."

"That's outrageous," said the Secretary of State.

"It was the method of Disraeli in procuring the Suez Canal and of President Jefferson in obtaining the Louisiana Purchase," said Wendover quietly. "In neither case was the legislature consulted until the object was accomplished. Mountjoy fancies he comes from the same mold—and he may be right."

"But even supposing he obtained this money," said the Secretary, "and I'm not for a moment conceding that he will, what chance does a tiny state like Grand Fenwick, lacking any technological development at all—a state that is utterly and completely agricultural—have of developing a rocket capable of going to the moon when we ourselves have failed time and again?"

"Mountjoy is a statesman of the European mold," said Wendover, "which means that his stated objective in putting forward a plan is not necessarily the main one, nor is it necessarily one which he really intends to implement."

"Put that in plain terms," said the Secretary of State testily.

"Well, sir," said Wendover, "you realize that I am guessing—but guessing from a knowledge of Mountjoy and the foreign and domestic problems of Grand Fenwick."

"In the final analysis we all guess," said the Secretary. "Go ahead."

"Mountjoy has been frustrated many times in the past in attempts to put into effect many programs he has had for the development of the Duchy," said Wendover. "These programs have included modernizing the highway system in the Duchy, putting up a tourist hotel of some distinction, revamping the plumbing in the castle of Grand Fenwick and putting modern plumbing in the houses of the people. Getting a hot bath in Grand Fenwick, sir, is still a three-hour project involving heating water in pots over an open fire. In all these projects he has been defeated by the Opposition, led by Mr. David Bentner who is the leader of what we will call the party of the people—not communist. Definitely anti-communist. But opposed to modern innovations that call for an increase in taxes.

"Now with regard to this application for a loan of five

million dollars to send a rocket to the moon, I would say that Mountjoy's real objective is to get funds (without an increase in domestic taxes) to revamp the whole plumbing arrangement in the castle of Grand Fenwick and also get a start on his highway program and his tourist hotel."

"Then why doesn't he apply for this kind of assistance which we are usually willing to give to backward nations?" interrupted the Secretary of State.

"You unwittingly hit on the reason when you spoke about 'backward nations,' sir," said Wendover. "No country likes to think of itself as a backward nation, particularly a country as proud of its history as Grand Fenwick. If Mountjoy applied directly to the United States for a loan to improve the —er—facilities in Grand Fenwick, he would bring down the wrath of the whole nation on his ears, for he would be making a national admission that his country was backward.

"He therefore hit upon this rocket pretext which lets him out and serves our purposes as well—as he explains in his letter."

"I don't agree that it serves our purposes at all," said the Secretary. "I don't agree with that in the slightest."

"I speak subject to your own more intimate knowledge of the whole situation, sir," said Wendover. "I don't pretend to be able to discuss the world picture with any degree of authority."

"Go ahead," said the Secretary. "Say what you have in mind."

"Well, as Mountjoy points out, it is part of the basic policy of this country to obtain, through the United Nations, international control of the moon, so that the quarrels of the earth are not extended to the moon, and the moon does not become a second Berlin, divided between East and West.

"However, if an agreement were achieved with the Russians on international control of the moon, it would really be bi-national control of the moon. It would be basically an agreement between two nations—the United States and Russia, each with its own point of view, and these points of view are likely to come into conflict at any moment. We might call it international control, but it wouldn't be. It would be basically another Berlin situation—East versus West.

"We, on our part, want to avoid that. We can't avoid it unless there is at least one other party involved. That would give it some kind of international flavor. If we could go before the United Nations and say that in our desire that the moon should be internationalized, we had advanced funds for research in getting a manned rocket to the moon to another nation outside our sphere of influence and with which we have no close connection, then we would have demonstrated our sincerity in attempting to get international lunar control. Mountjoy suggests this path though, as I have said, his real objective is probably to get a hot bath for himself and some decent roads in Grand Fenwick. But it is a path—an approach—which is very useful to us. It serves our purpose. And it serves it without detracting in the slightest from our national achievement if and when we get to the moon, or our national bargaining position."

"But Grand Fenwick?" said the Secretary of State. "Nobody is ever going to believe that we are serious in offering Grand Fenwick money to get to the moon. Grand Fenwick hasn't got a chance."

"They wouldn't believe it if we offered the money to any other small country," said Wendover. "But Grand Fenwick —Grand Fenwick is different."

"Why?" demanded the Secretary.

"Because of Dr. Kokintz," said Wndover. "He is the world's outstanding physicist and he lives in Grand Fenwick. There is just enough in that for people to suspect that he may be engaged in some kind of research regarding—well, rocket fuels. The man who invented the quadium bomb commands world respect. There is enough world respect for Dr. Kokintz for people to think—even Russia—that our offer to Grand Fenwick is sincere. And it would be sincere. It is a gesture only, of course. But it is a sincere gesture, costing only five million dollars which will do much to convince the world of our ardent desire to obtain a true international control of the moon—and of outer space when that field is opened up."

"And the fur coat?" asked the Secretary.

"That is undoubtedly a genuine objective of Mountjoy's," said Wndover. "But we have again to look for an ulterior motive, Mountjoy being, as I have stated, a statesman of the European kind. His ulterior motive, I would guess, is that with the presentation of the fur coat, which is tied in with the whole loan, he may be able to mitigate a great deal of the hostility which may develop when what he has done is discovered, because of the people's deep affection for the Duchess. As I said at the beginning, sir, I believe that Mountjoy has far exceeded his authority in applying for this sum. But if he gets what he asks for, and people start getting plenty of hot water in their homes and a good road through the Duchy and decent sanitation, and the Duchess gets a fur coat, then most of that hostility will disappear and he may well become for a while a national hero."

"You think we should grant this request for funds then?" asked the Secretary of State.

"Oh yes, sir," said Wendover. "Mountjoy is actually doing us a service. He makes it possible for us, with the expenditure of only five million dollars, to put the Russians in a position where they can hardly refuse true international exploration and control of space. That's not as much as one of our big rockets costs, I think, sir."

The Secretary was silent for a while, marveling at the mental subtleties of the Count of Mountjoy. There surely must be, he pondered, something in the business of diplomacy not merely as a career for one man but as a career for a whole family through scores of generations. "Lord," he said to himself, "if only we were not so handicapped in this country by a national love of being forthright and honest. What wonders we could achieve for the good of the world. Here is this trained statesman in a little country who writes me a letter on a single sheet of paper in which he carefully disguises his objectives and gains every one of them."

Aloud, he said to Wendover, "Give me a memorandum on this subject and I'll take it up with the President. You can recommend an outright grant. It would look better when we report to the United Nations if we say it was a gift with no strings attached. In any case, we have no hope of getting it back again. But five million dollars is ridiculous. It is too small. It would lack conviction when we go before the United Nations with the announcement. Better make it fifty million dollars. That would make it sound like a more genuine offer for funds for lunar research."

"Fifty million!" exclaimed Wendover. "But, sir, whatever would they do with the surplus?"

"That's their problem," said the Secretary, almost savagely. "They can rehouse everybody in Grand Fenwick for all I care, and buy them all automobiles. They may want to start a university over there. Anyway, it's their problem, as I say. My problem is not to jeopardize the success of this whole effort by being niggardly. In any case, we give so much money to nations which are wavering between us and the communists, it will be a pleasure to make a substantial gift to a nation whose principles are unshakable and coincide entirely with our own."

V

It was several days before Dr. Kokintz found time to develop the pictures he had taken of the bobolinks. During the interim he was busy with his inquiry into the physical and chemical properties of Pinot Grand Fenwick. In any case Dr. Kokintz was among those millions of people whose peculiarity it is that having taken a picture they cannot somehow bring themselves to go ahead and develop it. It was only under the gentle prodding of Tully Bascomb that he finally turned to the negatives, which he had had all the time in the pocket of his jacket, mixed the necessary chemicals and started to develop the plates.

The results were a disappointment. The center of each negative was fogged and there were little streaks all over the negatives, radiating out from the fogged area, which Dr. Kokintz assumed were made by scratches on the emulsion. These scratches, he believed, were his own fault, resulting from keeping the negatives in the plate holders so long in his pocket. The fogging of the center of each negative he laid to a light leak in the camera, but after examining the camera thoroughly he could find no light leak. In this predicament he called Tully to the darkroom where he was working.

"We must take the pictures of the bobolinks again," he said, showing him the negatives. "This was a bad batch of film. Light got in and ruined the negatives."

"It was all new film," said Tully. "None of it more than a month old. It's guaranteed for a year."

"Well, as you see, they are all spoiled," replied Kokintz. "Tomorrow we take some more shots."

"Okay," said Tully. "The bobolinks have established themselves in the big beech. I left the shelter from which we shot the pictures standing, so they have become accustomed to it. That will make it easier. They are most active at dawn, so we are likely to get our best pictures then."

"Yes," said Kokintz. "Yes. Meanwhile I will go over the camera again to ensure that there is nothing the matter with it."

When Tully had left, Kokintz slipped one of the fogged negatives into a light frame to study it. The fogged area in the center looked like a sunburst and its formation puzzled him. Out from it, like rays of the sun, came a series of streaks. The effect was not, on closer inspection, that of a normal light leak. He took a small jeweler's magnifying glass, set it on the negatives and peered through it.

"Very strange," he said to himself. "Very strange indeed. This is more like a radioactive effect. But the plates have not been near any radioactive material."

He thought about where the plates had been stored, recalled that he had had them in his jacket and his overcoat and started looking for the jacket, finding it thrown over the back of a chair. He took the jacket over to a workbench and emptied everything out of the pockets and was dismayed at the number of articles he found. There were eight mechanical pencils, each with a different colored lead, for Dr. Kokintz found the physical effort of writing a complete bore and to relieve the tedium wrote sometimes in red, sometimes in violet, sometimes in green and so on.

In addition there were several stubs of pencils he had picked up at one time or another and put into his pockets. There were numerous pieces of paper containing notes he had jotted down—some of them on birds, some of them equations involving the relationship between time and energy and time and space (Dr. Kokintz was deeply interested in the Einstein theory of the unified field but was beginning to suspect that an unknown dimension was lacking in the Einstein concept of the universe); there was a shriveled portion of an apple out of which he recalled he had taken a bite a week earlier, several packets of birdseed, an envelope containing a spoonful of sandy soil (to be analyzed for its mineral content), a yo-yo with a knot in the string (representing a promise made to a child the day before), and a letter from the President of the University of Pennsylvania (representing a promise to prepare a paper on the evidence of the spontaneous appearance of hydrogen atoms in outer space).

All these items he laid out on the bench before him, and then fell to examining the fogged negatives again. He glanced from the negatives to the assortment of articles he had taken from his pockets and then took them all, together with the spoiled negatives, into his darkroom.

Meanwhile the Count of Mountjoy impatiently awaited the reply to his letter to the United States Secretary of State. There were times when he was horrified at what he had done—at the extent to which he had exceeded his authorization by the Council of Freemen. At such times he saw himself tried for high treason, found guilty, and condemned to spend the rest of his life either as a political exile from Grand Fenwick or as a prisoner in the dungeons of the castle.

During his low periods he was exceedingly nervous and irritable and hard put to remain pleasant during his daily visits to the Duchess Gloriana. She noted his mood but concluded that it arose out of his anxiety over his son, Vincent of Mountjoy, a man of twenty-five years of age, who physically resembled his father the Count, being tall and lean and handsome, but bore no mental resemblance to him at all.

Vincent of Mountjoy took his mental qualities from his dead mother. He had no interest in political intrigue, all his love being reserved for engineering. He had, to satisfy his father, taken a degree in political science at Oxford, but had then studied engineering at the University of Sheffield in England—a university which the Count thought of in terms of a trade or technical school, an institution summoned into being to turn farmers' sons and butchers' boys into high-class mechanics.

"How the devil can they call themselves a university when they neglect the liberal arts and teach only techniques?" the Count demanded of his son when he learned that he was going to Sheffield after Oxford. "A university which deliberately prepares its students to earn a living is an outrageous fraud on education," the Count continued. "The proper aim of any university should be to prepare men to live like gentlemen—versed in the classics and part of the company of the immortals."

These arguments were without avail, Vincent took his bachelor of science in engineering at Sheffield, his master's degree in engineering at the University of London, and then his doctorate at the University of Pittsburgh, after which he returned to Grand Fenwick in obedience to his father, who wanted to make a statesman of him.

He was by no means happy there and would have left after a few weeks were he not counseled by Tully Bascomb to remain at least a year in the Duchy.

"You have been abroad a long time and know very little of Grand Fenwick," said Tully. "You ought to learn something about it. Stay a year. These offers of employment with United States Steel, General Electric, Aluminium Ltd. and the other big companies will still be available to you. But you owe Grand Fenwick and your father at least a year of your life. After all this is the nation of your birth and your father supplied you with the money for your education."

"But Grand Fenwick has nothing for me," said Vincent. "I'm completely out of place here. It will just be wasting a year—that's all."

"If you waste only one year out of your lifetime, and that to please your father, the wastage is very small," said Tully. "And who knows? Things may change in Grand Fenwick."

"If they haven't changed in six hundred years, they are hardly likely to change now," snapped Vincent. But he agreed to stay.

The decision was made a little more tolerable by Cynthia Bentner, daughter of David Bentner. She was pretty and good-natured and a very good listener. And although her education had not gone beyond that offered by the one public school in Grand Fenwick, she had a built-in common sense and ability to understand people that often surprised Vincent.

He spent a great deal of time in her company—sometimes walking with her and sometimes just sitting in the Bentner kitchen while she went about her work (her mother was dead so she was housekeeper to her father). He talked of all his problems, his ambitions and his frustrations, and sometimes he didn't talk at all but just found it restful to be with her.

Occasionally they quarreled. The quarreling was all on his part, the result of his frustrations. Once he called her "stupid" and said she had no more education than one of the sheep on the mountainside. "You have a brain but you don't do more with it than bake apple pies," he said at the close of one of these quarrels and left her. But he came back some days later and apologized.

"I didn't mean that about your education," he said. "I was angry with myself and took my anger out on you."

"But you are quite right," said Cynthia. "I'm not educated. I just had the ordinary education we have here in Grand Fenwick and I wasn't one of the top students. But I don't think everybody has to have a thorough education. There is a lot of work to be done in the world that doesn't require education. There are a lot of needs that have to be filled that don't call for education at all."

"Like what?" demanded Vincent.

"Like listening to people," said Cynthia. "There aren't any degrees given for it, but it is something someone has to do."

When she said this Vincent felt more ashamed of himself than ever. Cynthia seemed more of a complete human being than he was, and the thought first annoyed him and then humbled him. But the annoyance persisted, for Vincent of Mountjoy had this in common with his father—he did not like to be reminded by sensing the virtues of others that he himself was not perfect.

Whenever he thought of the brilliant career in engineering that lay ahead of him, he could see no place for Cynthia Bentner or Grand Fenwick in it. The two were strangely linked with each other, as if the girl were the personification of the country. And yet there were times when the thought of life without her to listen to him seemed the bleakest prospect. But he assured himself that this feeling arose out of boredom and sentimentality and he would be rid of it when freed of the year he had to spend in the Duchy.

Certainly some, though not the major, part of the Count's anxiety arose then from this relationship between his son and Cynthia Bentner. For the father was horrified at the thought of his son marrying so intellectually undistinguished a girl and, seeing the two of them more and more together, began to wonder whether he was wise in keeping Vincent in Grand Fenwick.

He was in a dilemma. If Vincent went away he would be lost to his father and Grand Fenwick for good. If he remained he might, the Count argued, ruin his life by marrying the wrong woman.

"It is a pity there is no one in the Duchy suitable for my son to marry," the Count said one day to Tully.

"Perhaps it is not such a pity," replied Tully. "Vincent is too young to marry yet."

"He's twenty-five years of age," retorted the Count.

"Yes, but he's emotionally immature," said Tully. "He still thinks of himself as the most important person in the world —the one who has to be suited in all things. That is the attitude of the perennial bachelor, who by his nature is emotionally immature.

"By the way we got some excellent pictures of the bobolinks at last. The first set of negatives were fogged though. Light leak."

"Congratulations," said the Count. "I've no doubt that's very important."

"It will cause a great deal of stir among ornithologists," said Tully. "Bobolinks are normally confined to the northeast coast of the United States."

"And a very good place for them too," replied the Count, and went off leaving Tully wondering why he was so edgy.

Awaiting then, in an agony of anxiety, the American reply to his note, the Count once more sought consolation from Dr. Kokintz. Others did not like to disturb the doctor when he was busy in his study, but the Count of Mountjoy felt himself bound by no such nicety and, having given a perfunctory knock, entered the scientist's apartments.

"Did you find my overcoat?" asked the scientist, who was busy at a bench littered with chemical glassware.

"Your overcoat?" echoed Mountjoy.

Kokintz turned and looked at him blankly. "You are not Mrs. Plummer," he said as if this was, in some way, the Count of Mountjoy's fault.

"No," said the Count.

"Well, then you cannot find my overcoat for me," said Kokintz. "And it is very important to find it. What did you do with it?"

"I?" said the Count surprised. "Nothing."

"Please find Mrs. Plummer and ask her what she did with my overcoat," said Dr. Kokintz. "If it is not the overcoat, then I do not understand it." The scientist was plainly distracted and, although the Count of Mountjoy resented being made into an errand boy, he went off in search of Mrs. Plummer and returned some minutes later with the overcoat and Mrs. Plummer, who took care of the scientist's wardrobe.

"Ah," said Dr. Kokintz. "If it is not the overcoat, it is a mystery."

"Well, it's a mystery to me right now," said the Count of Mountjoy. "Would you mind explaining what all the fuss is about?" For answer the scientist produced a number of developed photographic plates. They were all of them jet black without a single mark on them. "This one is the apple. Nothing," said Kokintz. "This one the yo-yo. Again nothing. This one my green pencil. Nothing again, as you can see."

"This still doesn't make any sense to me," said Mountjoy.

"There should be streaks on some of them," said Kokintz, "and there aren't. It must be the overcoat."

When Dr. Kokintz was perturbed in this manner, it was impossible for the Count to get any sense out of him.

"What did you do with this overcoat?" demanded Kokintz of Mrs. Plummer, holding up the overcoat.

"Sponged and pressed it," said Mrs. Plummer.

"Sponged and pressed it!" cried the doctor. "You may have sponged and pressed away a tremendous scientific discovery. You went through the pockets first?"

"Yes."

"You found anything?"

"There was one of them things (pointing to a photographic plate holder) and an old crumpled-up envelope."

"And what did you do with them?"

"I put that thing (again pointing to the plate holder) in the bottom of the closet. And I threw the envelope down there with it."

"Please get both of them immediately," said Kokintz, plainly very anxious.

Mrs. Plummer went off and returned with the two oddly assorted items. Without another word Dr. Kokintz took the plate holder and went into his darkroom, where he remained for some time. The Count of Mountjoy dismissed Mrs. Plummer, who went away somewhat ruffled but recovered her good spirits by relating to her fellow servants that Dr. Kokintz was up to his experiments again and might bring the whole castle down about their ears before the night was out.

The Count awaited the return of the scientist from the darkroom, but he was a long time coming and in any case was concerned with incomprehensible problems dealing with fogged photographic plates. The Count therefore left to brood in his own quarters about his own problems, first among them the reply from the United States Secretary of State.

VI

Mail for the Duchy of Grand Fenwick usually came through France, being delivered at the Duchy's borders by a bus running from Pontarliers to Baume des Dames. It may have been rushed across the world by jet plane at a speed of ten miles a minute or more. But it reached Grand Fenwick at ten miles an hour or less carried in a flat-nosed Renault bus which wheezed and shuddered up and down the piedmont country skirting the Grand Fenwick border.

The driver of the bus had a fine Gallic disregard for schedules and punctuality. He looked on the compiling of a schedule by the owners of the bus as, first an attempt to enslave him by binding his movements to the dictates of a clock and, secondly, a piece of supreme folly since even if, being in a good mood, he wished to abide by the schedule, the Renault could not be relied upon to co-operate.

Added to this, the bus sometimes left before the mail for Grand Fenwick arrived at Pontarliers. Or the bus driver, in a fit of pique, decided not to carry any mail for Grand Fenwick on that day. And so the delivery of mail to the Duchy was haphazard and this added considerably to the torments of the Count of Mountjoy, awaiting his reply from the Secretary of State of the United States of America.

When the mail came on the bus, it was deposited in a letter box which was attached to a stone pillar on the Duchy's border where the road into the Duchy met the Pontarliers-Baume des Dames highway.

Grand Fenwick had not got a mailman of its own. The system was for anyone who happened to be passing the mailbox to take a look inside and see if there were any letters. If there were, they brought the letters back and delivered them to the addresses.

In short, anybody in Grand Fenwick who happened to be near the mailbox was the mailman, and quite often people put letters in their pockets and forgot to deliver them for a day or two, though no one took umbrage at this.

It was not to be wondered at then that when the Count of Mountjoy got his reply from the Secretary of State, it had been two days in the pocket of a farmer who had picked it up from the mailbox and who, having a sick cow on his hands (he had gone to the mailbox to get a bottle of physic for the cow for which he had sent away), administered first to the cow and then, belatedly, brought the letter to the Count.

Mountjoy snatched it hastily from the man, dismissed him with an impatient wave of his hands and hurried trembling to his study, where he opened the letter. The first thing his eyes lit on in the letter was the figure $50,000,000. He stared at it, his heart pounding wildly.

"Fifty million dollars," he cried. "There must be a mistake!" He snatched up the envelope to check the address, for the wild thought crossed his mind that the communication was not intended for Grand Fenwick but for Italy or France or some other larger nation which by reason of its size would be in need of this monstrous sum.

But the envelope was addressed to him; and turning once more to the letter, he found that the sum of $50,000,000 was written out in words after the figures, so there was no possibility even of a typist's error. Calming his nerves, he forced himself to read the letter through word by word, and as he read, his initial panic at the thought that he had put Grand Fenwick into debt to the tune of $50,000,000 subsided, to be replaced, when he was through with the reading, with triumph and exultation.

The letter stated that the request for a loan of funds with which to start research on the problem of sending a manned rocket to the moon had been given careful consideration and the United States, anxious to avoid any suggestion of monopoly or of national ambition in the exploration of space, was pleased to grant the sum of $50,000,000 to the Duchy for this purpose.

The letter continued:

The Government of the United States is completely sincere in its desire to make the exploration of space a project for all mankind. It is therefore the Government's wish that this money should be considered an outright gift of funds, without any obligation for repayment either of the principal or of interest on the principal.

"Great Heavens!" cried Mountjoy. "What a magnificent nation! I ask for sufficient funds with which to build a shower-bath and I receive enough for a marble tub with gold fittings and mink around the edges. God bless America—the hope of the world and the solace of all." He was highly excited and deeply moved by this tremendous American generosity and in this mood he cried, "We must defend them. Such a nation must not be allowed to perish through the schemings of the baser sort. I will send a strong note to Russia on behalf of the United States immediately, firmly placing Grand Fenwick beside that magnificent country in its stand on Berlin."

He was so delighted with the prospect of having, as a result of this astonishing American generosity, all the hot and cold running water needed in every part of the castle, that he strode swiftly into the small stone chamber where the hipbath in which he was accustomed to bathe was placed on the floor and gave it a hearty kick. The hipbath had just been filled with water for him; the kick split the ancient seam in the bottom and the water cascaded over the floor.

"Bah!" cried the Count of Mountjoy. "I will soon be through with you and your outrageous indignities."

Such enormous good news the Count could by no means keep to himself. There were two people with whom he could share it immediately. The first was of course Dr. Kokintz, to whom the Count always turned whether in depression, boredom or excitement. He rushed to Kokintz' apartments but Kokintz was busy with photographic plates in which he had recently been taking an astonishing interest.

"Fifty million dollars, my dear Doctor," cried the Count, waving the letter. "We shall have everything that we need here."

The scientist looked at the Count absently over his rimless and thick glasses, nodded his head, and went on with his fussing with the plates without a word. It was plain that he had not understood what was said to him. Rather than attempt to penetrate the thick fog of concentration that surrounded Dr. Kokintz, Mountjoy left him, a little piqued, to find Tully Bascomb and break the news to him.

Bascomb's reaction, however, was not at all what the Count had anticipated.

Mountjoy related all the details of his correspondence with the Secretary of State, and concluded jubilantly, "Just think, my friend, how brilliantly I have succeeded—there is a lesson in statesmanship for you. Not five million dollars but fifty million dollars. Not chromium-plated faucets but solid-gold faucets and bathtubs of onyx if we wish. We can make Grand Fenwick the tourist paradise of the world. And of course an Imperial Russian Sable fur coat for Her Grace. It is beyond all my wildest expectations. Of course, I am going to need your help in explaining how all this came about to the Council of Freemen. I must plead guilty to exceeding my—er—instructions from them. But the reward in this case certainly justifies my little deception."

"Let me see that letter," said Tully, and taking it from Mountjoy, he read it through with great deliberation.

"This letter says that the money is given us to spend on

research aimed at sending a manned rocket to the moon," he said when he had done. "There isn't a word in it about spending the money on anything else."

"Of course not, my dear fellow," said Mountjoy. "That's statesmanship—diplomacy. One never sets forth the real reasons and motivations in exchanges of this kind. I ask for the money for rocket research, providing an excellent opportunity to the United States for granting it; they give us the money, officially for rocket research, but they don't care at all what we spend it on. They get fifty million dollars' worth of excellent propaganda, being able to go before the world, in all sincerity, and show that they have made a practical effort toward internationalizing the conquest of space. We get fifty million dollars' worth of bathtubs. So both sides are pleased and a solid step toward breaking the East-West deadlock on space exploration is achieved."

Tully shook his head. "It won't do," he said. "We in Grand Fenwick haven't yet come to the point when we cheat people—when we obtain money under false pretenses, particularly from the United States of America, which is a nation with strong and worthy ideals and a nation far younger than we are. We should be helping the United States and advising and supporting it, as a younger nation than we are. Not cheating it. We must send the money back."

"But, my dear fellow," cried the Count in deep distress, "you can't do that to my good friend, the American Secretary of State. You can't let him down in this manner. When he offers us fifty million dollars of his own free will—it was entirely voluntary on his part for I suggested only five million —you can't turn around and tell him that you don't want it! Just think for a moment what you are proposing. Nobody has ever rejected an offer of American money. It's absolutely unheard of. It would produce some kind of a world crisis—perhaps irreparably shake the faith of world financiers in the American dollar, with disastrous results to the whole of the Western economy.

"He has offered us the money in good faith, with every expectation that we would accept it. It would be a dreadful breach of faith not to co-operate by accepting the money. It is the only honorable thing to do."

"He offered us the money for the express purpose of rocket research," said Tully obstinately. "It will be spent on rocket research, or returned. That's final."

"You don't understand at all," said the Count of Mountjoy, quite exasperated. "The trouble is that you have been ruined in your youth by being brought up to think in a straightforward manner and never as a statesman. 'Honesty is the best policy' is a text you have copied out so many times in your youth that it has quite ruined your mind. Honesty—frankness—is not in the slightest commensurate with wise statesmanship. If people knew everything that was going on in their governments, everything that was planned for them in the future, they'd lose their nerve. If they were brought face to face with every crisis their governments face every day, there would be national hysteria followed by anarchy. Governments are elected so that nations may prosper while really not knowing what is going on at all. That is the art of successful government.

"Nor can governments carry on their business effectively with each other by telling each other frankly what are their policies and their objectives.

"Good heavens, what a monstrous handicap such an arrangement would prove.

"No plan for national advancement could ever be put into effect, for it would be immediately seized upon and thwarted by some other nation. Deceit, my dear boy, is the very lubricant of the machinery of international diplomacy. It is by subterfuge that the whole complicated mechanism works smoothly, and nothing is so embarrassing for governments as to be brought together at round-table conferences, charged with doing that one thing which cannot be done if progress is to be achieved—talk frankly to each other.

"It is for this reason that huge staffs have to draw up the agendas for such time-wasting devices and whole corps of experts have to provide the chiefs of state with a mass of information on all kinds of questions which can be dragged in to obscure the objectives which each wishes to achieve.

"At the end of these conferences (and there have, as you know, been a plethora of them since World War Two) all that can be announced is that progress has been made, and a cordial atmosphere has prevailed throughout the talks.

"Then the whole thing is put back where it belongs, in the hands of experienced statesmen who, proceeding by the time-honored techniques of indirection, achieve what is best for their countries. Meanwhile the public is assured that all is well and tensions are relaxed.

"So you must see that it is an outrageous abuse of the trust of another nation to state plainly what is one's objective in any negotiation. And it is certainly intolerable when a loan is granted to use the money for the purposes officially advanced for giving the loan. It is quite well understood that these loans and grants are to be put to whatever purpose best suits the nation receiving them. And in our case, plumbing comes far ahead of rocketry."

"From whom does this money come in the first place?" asked Tully, who was somewhat bemused by this snowstorm of diplomatic interpretation.

"From the American taxpayer, of course," replied the Count. "Something less than a dollar from each one of them over the period of a year, I'd say."

"Well, do you suppose that the American taxpayer would be willing to part with fifty million dollars so you can have a hot bath?" Tully demanded.

"He certainly wouldn't," said Mountjoy. "But that doesn't matter. He doesn't *know* about it and rests content in the thought that the money is being spent in rocket research and will take some of the menace out of the exploration of space."

"Then we have no right to deceive the American taxpayers," said Tully.

"Good heavens!" cried the Count of Mountjoy. "Why are you suddenly so virtuous? The American taxpayer's government has been deceiving him for years, lending money to South American dictators, for instance, which the taxpayer thought was being spent on South American peasants. Besides, his own Secretary of State agrees with the deceit. He knows that it is good for the American taxpayer. And it *is* good for him. It takes the rivalry out of the space race by introducing a third power. That makes the world safer for the American taxpayer, which is the proper objective of the American government. And we get our bathtubs."

"It won't do," said Tully. "This money is going to be spent for the purpose for which it is officially given in this letter, or I will oppose its acceptance, denounce you before the Council of Freemen for exceeding your instructions and thereby betraying the trust reposed in you, and insist the money be returned to the United States of America. With Bentner on my side, that would mean that you are thrown out of office and he would take over as the Prime Minister."

"God forbid!" cried Mountjoy with deep fervor.

"Well, there it is," said Tully. "Take it or leave it."

Mountjoy had been long in the merciless arena of politics. He had seen many otherwise brilliant men ruined because they did not know how to turn defeat into compromise. He knew he was defeated now. But he had a few weapons left and with them he could perhaps achieve a compromise.

"Young man," he said gravely, "I am going to give you a lesson in ethics and statesmanship that students of political science would come from all parts of the world to hear.

So listen carefully. I will take as my text the subject of honesty as it affects the present situation. You talk of honesty, but like the greater number of people, you think of honesty primarily in terms of money. Yours is a mercantile point of view and a poor one. There is an honesty of friendship and an honesty of principle. There is an honesty and an honor among thieves and an honesty and honor among statesmen and politicians, though the vulgar may jeer at the concept.

"You see here only fifty million dollars which is a sum of money, and are concerned that it be honestly spent. But there is also here another sum—a sum of trust—which cannot be expressed in money. It is the trust which the United States of America reposes in us to accept this money and so help them in this plan to internationalize the exploration of space and the conquest of the moon.

"That plan, I agree, was mine. I put it forward in all good faith to the Secretary of State. He has accepted it in all good faith.

"It would be dishonest to the point of treachery for us to withdraw now—far more dishonest than the misappropriation of sums of money far greater than that with which we are concerned.

"If we withdraw, we have spent our credit of honor with America. We have proposed a plan to them and when they have accepted it, we have reneged on them. We become, in matters of faith, untrustworthy and bankrupt, now and for all time.

"In the final analysis, my boy, the strength and safety of nations rests not on treaties or grand agreements at conferences, but on the trust each nation reposes in the other. The United States trusts us to accept this money so that they can go forward with their plan of an announcement of the grant before the United Nations to promote the internationalization of the conquest of space. We cannot; we must not let them down."

This little homily had some effect upon Tully. "I am not proposing to send the money back," he said slowly. "I am merely insisting that it be spent on rocket research."

"I am relieved to hear that you are not thinking of returning it," said the Count of Mountjoy. "We reach a basic agreement here then. There remains only the matter of expenditure. You are aware, of course, that considerable benefit will accrue to our people by the expenditure of such an enormous sum within our boundaries—if the expenditure is wisely directed."

"What do you mean by wisely directed?" asked Tully.

"Well, if the money is put into rocket research, there is no benefit to anyone in Grand Fenwick. Dr. Kokintz alone is employed and at the present moment his requirements seem to run to nothing more than a few photographic plates.

"If, however, not all the money is spent on rocket research, but a reasonable proportion upon works of benefit to all the people—work in which they can be employed and which will bring others into the country to spend money . . ."

"Meaning roads, a hotel and plumbing," interrupted Tully.

"We can skip the hotel," said Mountjoy. "At least for the present. But if the plumbing facilities of the castle were modernized with some portion of the money, and perhaps one wing set aside with facilities for tourists—rather like the Portuguese have done with some of their castles—then there would be an immediate and a lasting benefit to the people of Grand Fenwick.

"I would point out that we are not likely ever again in all our history to have such funds available. We can do this now. Or we can never do it. And much as I respect your feelings for the American taxpayer, I am sure I don't have to remind you that your first concern must be for the Grand Fenwick taxpayers."

"How much?" asked Tully.

"Five millions," said the Count without batting an eyelid. "The sum for which I originally asked. What you and Kokintz do with the forty-five million dollars for which I did not ask, I leave entirely to you."

Tully thought about this for a while and then said, "All right. Five million for the castle and the road. The rest for rocket research."

"Agreed," said the Count and they shook hands. He had not snatched victory from the jaws of defeat. He had done what is often more difficult—snatched compromise from the jaws of disaster. He was very pleased with himself.

VII

The announcement of a free grant of $50,000,000 to the Duchy of Grand Fenwick for research on sending a manned rocket to the moon was made at a meeting of the General Assembly of the United Nations and produced the only sensation of an extraordinarily dull session of that unwieldy but fast-growing body.

Prior to the announcement there had been an open discussion of the problem of internationalizing space exploration—to the utter befuddlement of the representatives of some of the younger nations. These, sent at enormous expense to New York from remote parts of Equatorial Africa, each nursing some acute problem concerning its claim to a gold mine or a section of a muddy river, or a thousand square miles of jungle into which few but pygmies had ever penetrated, found the great nations of the world at loggerheads over who should own the moon.

To many of them it all appeared utter nonsense and to some of them downright sacrilegious, it being held by some, not necessarily by the envoys but by the more simple of the people they represented, that the moon was an egg laid by a giant fish which swam through the sky, its wake being the Milky Way. It would go hard with these envoys, indeed, on returning to their people to report that Russia and the United States were quarreling for possession of this sacred fish egg, and one envoy sent a touching note in duplicate to the United States and the Soviet Union, asking that they leave the sacred fish egg alone, but assist in reducing beriberi, which afflicted twenty per cent of the people in his small country.

The debate, then, over the moon had occupied much of the business of this particular meeting of the General Assembly and the United States delegate had neatly maneuvered the Russian delegate into a trap. He had talked long and with sincerity about the American ideal of internationalization of space research and the Russian delegate, leaping to his feet, had shouted, "The words of the United States of America are, as usual, and to nobody's surprise, at a complete variance with her actions. Here we have millions of words spoken about international co-operation in this area, but what are the actions of the leading capitalist nation?

"Well, I turn to figures officially published by the Government of the United States and these figures tell me that in the past year the United States of America in an accelerated program has expended two billion dollars on research aimed at getting first to the moon. So while the delegate of the United States talks here of a joint international venture, the Government of the United States is pouring vast sums of money and vast amounts of time and energy into getting first to the moon, so that it can claim the moon for its own territory.

"But we, who represent the aspirations of the working peoples of the world and are their true guardians and whose astronauts have already on several occasions circled the earth, will not permit this extension of the decadent capitalist philosophy into space, and on behalf of mankind are ourselves rushing plans to get first to the moon.

"In fact, we have already some years ago landed a rocket on the moon with painted on its side the flag of our country—representing, of course, the working people of all countries . . ."

"Workers of the moon—unite," murmured the British delegate and smiled charmingly at the Russian, who glowered back at him.

"I am afraid I have to correct the figures quoted by my colleague from the Soviet Union," interrupted the American delegate, "but let me hasten to add that in this case he is not to be blamed for his error. The correct figure is not two billion dollars, but two billion and fifty million dollars."

"That's even worse," said the Russian and he looked around at the delegates of all the new African nations, "but in the interests of the workers we will match it."

"I am glad to hear of that," said the American delegate mildly, "and hope that the Soviet Union will not go back on the promise just made. We have indeed spent two billion on our own research. And we have given fifty million dollars as an outright grant to the Duchy of Grand Fenwick to conduct independent research of its own accord, without any control by ourselves or reference to ourselves. We have done this to internationalize the space race. If I may quote a Texas proverb to my Russian colleague, we have put our money where our mouth was.

"May I invite the Soviet Union to do the same? We have had a promise before this assembly a moment ago that the Soviet Union would match our efforts. Perhaps they will announce now to what nation, independent of themselves, they will make a similar grant for this purpose."

The Russian delegate was utterly dumbfounded by the way the tables were so suddenly turned upon him. He consulted hurriedly with his colleague, then scooped up a bundle of papers on the table before him, and departed, followed by his assistants, leaving the United States the clear victor in the whole debate.

When the Russian had gone, the United States delegate expanded on the purpose and terms of the grant to Grand Fenwick. He admitted that the idea had been proposed by Grand Fenwick. He said that ordinarily such an application would have been turned down were it not for the fact that Grand Fenwick possessed in the person of Dr. Kokintz one of the world's outstanding physicists. The United States was happy to facilitate the work of so great a man on a project of importance to all the world. He said that the

world would without a doubt rejoice that this genius of
science was now able to work on this problem, that the
United States would render all the aid it could to his re-
searches, while leaving him completely free to work as he
wished.

The delegate concluded by circulating among the members of the Assembly extracts of the relevant correspondence between the Duchy of Grand Fenwick and the United
States of America on the subject. (These extracts included,
of course, the letter from the Count of Mountjoy, but the
reference to the fur coat for Her Grace Gloriana XII had
naturally been left out.)

The announcement produced a sensation.

The delegate from Iraq gained the floor to express on behalf of his government its confidence in the sincerity of
the United States, and his little speech was received with
such thunderous applause that it was plain the whole Assembly shared the sentiment. The victory then was complete,
and the Soviet Union was immediately placed in the position of matching the American gesture or devising some
propaganda line to offset its effect.

In Grand Fenwick itself, the effect was not so happy.
The Count of Mountjoy had summoned a meeting of the
Council of Freemen in the Jericho chamber of the castle
to announce the grant, timing the meeting to coincide with
the announcement by the United States before the General
Assembly.

The Duchess Gloriana had, of course, been informed privately of the grant and was appalled. She was very glad indeed to know that she could have her fur coat and that it
would not cost the people of Grand Fenwick anything. But
it worried her to have such a huge sum of money put into
the treasury of the nation, and it took all the persuasions
of Mountjoy to assure her that no terrible disaster would
befall her country as a result of this sudden access of riches.

"Your Grace," said Mountjoy, not without a touch of
revenge, "you admonished me to think big. I thought big.
The United States thought bigger. Now let us prove equal
to the enormous opportunities so unexpectedly put before
us. With this money we will make Grand Fenwick the
tourist paradise of the world. We will have a hotel which,
for service and cuisine, will rival the Ritz in Lisbon. We
will have an enormous influx of money from visitors, and
in a few years fifty million dollars will perhaps be but a
trifle of our national budget."

"Bobo, do you really think it will be all right?" asked
Gloriana seriously. "I mean we are not cheating anyone?

And Grand Fenwick isn't going to become so prosperous that it—well, that it's all changed and ruined?"

"Do not concern yourself, Your Grace," said the Count, and happily recalling a phrase of Sir Winston Churchill's he added, "I have not become Your Grace's Prime Minister to preside over the dissolution of Grand Fenwick." Then he left, tall, silver-haired and stately, and Gloriana, watching him go, sighed and wondered how many rulers were so well served by so handsome (although elderly) a man.

Mountjoy had for a time considered breaking the news of the grant to Bentner in advance of the official announcement to the Council of Freemen. He decided not to do so, suspecting that Bentner by his very nature would oppose the acceptance of the grant and might, in some bumbling way, ruin the whole arrangement. But he determined to have a private conference with Bentner after the official announcement in which he would hint at certain aspects of the use of the funds which would result in a larger proportion being devoted to Mountjoy's own purposes. It would be better for the success of this plan if the idea came from Bentner as leader of the Labor Party.

Bentner did oppose the grant.

He was flabbergasted when it was announced at the meeting. He made it clear that in his opinion Grand Fenwick's business began and ended at the borders of Grand Fenwick and by no means extended into the solitudes of space to embrace the moon.

He saw, and rightly, the Machiavellian mind of the Count of Mountjoy in the whole offer, and he was outraged at the way in which the Count had utterly exceeded his license from the Council and under the guise of obtaining a fur coat had plunged Grand Fenwick into the cockpit of international affairs, there to cut, as he saw it, a ridiculous figure before the whole world. No smooth phrases of the Count's were equal to the task of quelling Bentner's wrath.

"Traitor," he cried again and again, pointing his finger at the Prime Minister, and his most damning indictment came when he asked the Council of Freemen what confidence they could put in a premier who called them into session only to deceive them, who utterly abused the authority conferred upon him and who used the ancient Parliament of Grand Fenwick as a front behind which he carried on his own secret and personal form of government.

"The action of the Count of Mountjoy, the deliberate deceit he has practiced on us all demands his impeachment," stormed Bentner. And he there and then offered a motion that Mountjoy be impeached for abusing his position as Prime Minister.

There were twelve members of the Council and the vote was six for and six against impeachment. The deciding vote lay with Tully Bascomb and he voted against the measure and so the Count escaped this, the most perilous passage, of his whole political career.

But there was as bad to come. Bentner, not to be rebuffed, demanded that the Parliament be dissolved and that a general election be held since the government, headed by Mountjoy, had lost the confidence of Parliament. This vote carried, by eight to four, and Mountjoy had the unpleasant task of tendering his resignation to the Duchess Gloriana and setting a date for a general election.

The general election was held in a hurry, for the ripening vines required the attention of the vineyard workers and spring-lambing time was in full swing.

But despite the hurry it was furiously fought with public meetings held every evening, Bentner denouncing Mountjoy and his party as power-mad, determined to crush the workers of Grand Fenwick with grandiose schemes which would ruin the nation. "This madman will crush the nation under the weight of the moon," Bentner exclaimed in one of his more inspired moments. And for the rest of the campaign he referred to Mountjoy as the "Moonstruck Meddler."

Mountjoy was more subtle. He did no campaigning at all, contenting himself by mentioning to the castle servants who brought him his bath water up three hundred steps each day, that they would be relieved of this onerous task if the election went in his favor and he was allowed to use a portion of the American funds to install proper plumbing in the castle.

The word went around and with it the hope of plumbing in the houses of all the people of Grand Fenwick. The agricultural workers were solidly behind Bentner; strongly suspicious of the American offer and its effect on their country. Their wives, laboring with kettles to fill wooden tubs in which to do their laundry, were solidly behind Mountjoy. Mountjoy's party carried the election handsomely, so that it might be said that washtubs set Grand Fenwick on its way to the moon—as strange a development of history as the world has ever witnessed.

When the returns of what came to be known as the Lunar Election were in, Mountjoy's party had a solid majority in the Council of Freemen of three votes and Bentner was dazed to discover that women, who in Grand Fenwick had no vote, were yet capable of swinging an election.

"I could have warned you of this outcome before, my good man," Mountjoy informed him loftily when the returns were in. "There has never been a time or a country in history when women have not had a vote—even though they may officially be unable to cast a ballot. Since balloting was first devised, men may have cast the ballots but women have always told them how to do it. But do not be disturbed. I can be of some help to you and you can be of some help to me in the grave business that lies ahead."

Much chastened, Bentner was inclined to listen to the counsel of Mountjoy.

"As matters now stand," said Mountjoy, "Bascomb intends that forty-five million dollars are to be literally flung into the sky in a ridiculous attempt to get to the moon. Only five million are left to benefit the people of Grand Fenwick in works of one kind or another. If we work wisely together, we should be able to reverse these figures.

"It would have been much easier, by the way, if you hadn't called for that general election when you did. If you hadn't done so, you might have been able to call for one after accepting the money and campaigned on the issue of getting forty-five million dollars for the workers of Grand Fenwick, leaving the five million dollars for the moon. In which case you would undoubtedly have won. You must learn, Bentner, in politics, while publicly challenging your opposition on every occasion, to work closely with him behind the scenes, as quite often the opposition has precisely the same aims as yourself."

"But I didn't want any part of the money," said Bentner, "and I still don't."

"You must learn to be a realist and not a dreamer," said Mountjoy. "Nobody has ever won an election by demanding that the voters turn down an offer of fifty million dollars. You were beaten at the start. Your proper objective should have been to get as much of the fifty million as you could for your party. However, as I say, we can perhaps work together on the matter. If, for instance, you were to introduce a motion when we have accepted the funds that a larger portion be spent in Grand Fenwick and less on the moon, my party would support you and the motion would be unanimously carried. That would considerably restore your political prestige here."

"But I don't want any part of the money," repeated Bentner. "I know what you're after with your highway and hotel program. You'll ruin the country. And I don't want to have anything to do with ruining the country. I like it the way it is."

"Well," said Mountjoy with a sigh, "it seems to me that I will have to take over the leadership of both parties in Grand Fenwick since you are intent upon deserting the working people. It will be somewhat difficult to supply my own Opposition but I have no doubt I can manage it." He left Bentner to think the matter over and Bentner, lacking other counsel, consulted with his daughter, Cynthia.

"If Mountjoy has his way," he said, "it's going to mean rising wages and rising prices and all the troubles of inflation. The Grand Fenwick pound is as solid now as the Swiss franc. But let wages start rising and groups of foreign workers come into the country building highways and hotels and putting in plumbing, and then let them be followed by hordes of tourists and our pound won't be worth a Swiss centime. It's happened elsewhere and it can happen here. That Mountjoy is a villain. He'll ruin this country with his scheming."

"If you think it will ruin the country," said Cynthia quietly, "it seems to me that you can't avoid accepting the money, but there is nothing to prevent you throwing it away."

"Throwing it away?" echoed Bentner. "You can't take fifty million dollars and just dump it out with the garbage. People would pick it up and start spending it and everything I fear would happen."

"You have to throw it somewhere where they can't get it," said Cynthia, busy with her ironing. "About a quarter of a million miles away."

"Meaning?" asked Bentner, who was not at his most acute.

"You have to throw it away on the moon," said his daughter. "Just insist that every penny of it is spent on this rocket research and when the rocket is made and all the money is tied up in it, then fire it off to the moon and you have no more money problems.

"They have been doing that in America for years," she added, "but then I expect they have so much money there that getting rid of it is a problem. And if the money is spent on this rocket, then I think Vincent will stay here. It would give him something to use his engineering training on instead of taking one of those big jobs in America."

"You want him to stay?" asked Bentner, hardly aware that any relationship existed between his daughter and the Count of Mountjoy's son.

"Yes," said Cynthia. "I do. And if it means building a rocket to go to the moon to keep him here, then that's what has to be done."

Bentner became conscious, and not for the first time, of

depths in his daughter beyond his knowledge. He began to feel a little uneasy and, recalling what had happened to him during the recent elections, he said, "Cynthia, did you have anything to do with Mountjoy winning that last election?"

Cynthia turned the shirt she was ironing over, spread the collar carefully, and ran the iron over it. Her father noted that she was blushing a little at the base of her neck.

"I did mention to some of the other women that it would be nice to have hot and cold water in the houses and maybe washing machines," she said.

"You mean that you took a part in defeating your own father?" demanded Bentner.

"Well," said Cynthia, "it was very important that you lose the election because if you won, the money would have been turned down and then Vincent would have gone to the United States and perhaps met somebody over there and I would never have seen him again."

"Did the Count of Mountjoy put you up to this?" demanded Bentner.

"He thought he did," said Cynthia, "but I had worked it out for myself before. Women have a lot of time to think when they are ironing, and men are always kept busy at things that don't let them think. Besides, when a woman is in love, she has to do everything she can to keep her man for herself."

"You mean that you are in love with Vincent of Mountjoy?" demanded Bentner. "How long has this been going on?"

"Let's see," said Cynthia calmly. "I'm twenty-two now, so it's seventeen years. When I was five he hit me on the head with a little red mallet and that's when I fell in love with him, and I've been in love with him ever since." She folded the shirt down neatly and turned to another, and David Bentner looked at her in astonishment and awe, bemused at the issues which, all unknown to him, a prime contender, had been involved in the general election.

"I am on your side now," said Cynthia after a while. "I think you ought to see that every penny of that money is spent on the rocket. That would keep Vincent here longer and give me a better chance with him. I don't think he would be much interested, with all his degrees, in installing plumbing or even building highways. But designing a rocket —that would be a big challenge."

So it was that the Count of Mountjoy, far from obtaining Bentner's aid in securing more of the money for spending in Grand Fenwick, found Bentner insisting that every penny of it be spent on lunar research, including the five million which Tully Bascomb had agreed should be earmarked for the Count's purposes.

It took him some little time to discover the real source of this stubborn opposition.

VIII

By May of 1968 three nations were fully entered in the race for the moon. They were the Union of Soviet Socialist Republics with an area of something over 8,300,000 square miles, the United States of America with an area of around 3,000,000 square miles and the Duchy of Grand Fenwick, whose area may be put precisely at 23 square miles and 17 acres. The odds, if size were to be regarded as a factor, were obviously heavily loaded in favor of the Union of Soviet Socialist Republics and indeed that nation hoped to offset the price of shoes and the lack of privacy among its people by being first to the moon. As the British representative at the United Nations, who was something of a wit, remarked over his whisky and soda in the delegates' lounge, "Our Communist friends have taken over the old slogan about 'Pie in the Sky.' Well, we mustn't complain. We got plenty of mileage out of it ourselves in our day."

Nobody outside of those directly engaged, knew how close to a moon landing the Russians were. They had achieved some magnificent feats in space. Their astronauts had not only circumnavigated the earth several times, but their scientists had put several space capsules in orbit around the moon as satellites. The next step was plainly a space platform circling the moon from which a local rocket-launching could be made to the moon's surface and back again to the space platform. And yet for a full year there had been no great advance in the Russian program, which seemed to have entered, after a brilliant start, a period of stalemate.

With the United States, matters were somewhat better. The United States had come belatedly into the space race, and had proceeded cautiously. There had been a lot of service bickering and infighting which had held up rocket development. But the American program gathered momentum as the months and years went by, and the handicap of having had to work initially with underpowered rockets with a thrust of scarcely two hundred tons was now paying dividends.

In the days of the small-thrust rockets, American scientists had been forced to miniaturize all their instruments and cut down on weight in every department, while Russia, with a rocket developing a thrust of five hundred tons, had been under no such handicap. The result was that the United States rocket designers had become experts at weight reduction without sacrifice of efficiency. They now had rockets with a thrust equal to if not greater than those of Russia. The Saturn Rocket Mark II developed a whopping 1500 tons of thrust and could carry on its nose a three-man space craft which could be put into orbit around the moon (on which the rocket itself would land) rejoining the rocket for the return to earth after a full photographic survey of the moon's surface had been made.

Grand Fenwick had Dr. Kokintz, $50,000,000 and a minor political crisis, as the Labor party insisted that the full $50,000,000 be shot to the moon in the interests of the nation, and Mountjoy found for $5,000,000 of it for bathtubs —also in the interests of the nation.

Nobody in Grand Fenwick had any idea of how to start to get to the moon though all the people for a while had a sense of great importance that their country should have been selected for such a project. The farmers talked wisely to each other about what should be the first thing done when a man landed on the moon's surface. Most agreed that a flag should be planted somewhere, but after that they were at something of a loss, for as far as they knew the moon was just a large lump of rock floating up there in the sky and it would be impossible to raise sheep on it or plant vines. It seemed then that after planting a flag on the moon, the next thing to do would be to get back to earth again as quickly as possible, and when the novelty of the thing had worn off, the whole project, while fascinating to the children, seemed rather silly to the older people, who took to remarking wisely that no good would come of it.

Mountjoy was, of course, pleased with this development. He believed that all he had to do was bide his time and the whole of Grand Fenwick would be behind him and he would be able to get the major portion of the funds for the various projects for the development of the country which were so dear to his heart.

But Mountjoy had reckoned without Dr. Kokintz, who for the past several weeks had been working with the photographic plates he had exposed in attempting to get pictures of the two bobolinks. (The bobolinks had nested in the big beech and the female was sitting on the eggs, which pleased the scientist enormously.)

One day he sought an audience with Gloriana and Tully, saying he had something very important to tell them.

"If it is about the bobolinks," said Gloriana to Tully, "maybe it can wait until tomorrow. I have to get my hair washed this afternoon and you know what a business that is."

"I don't think it's about the bobolinks," said Tully. "When Dr. Kokintz says it's something important, it could be birds, but it could be something like Einstein's theory of the unified field. He has a queer idea of what is important. I think we ought to see him."

Gloriana sighed, and the two of them called on the doctor in his apartments since he had asked if they would see him there.

They found him at ease in a large leather chair and he seated them courteously and begged them not to be disturbed by the festoons of developed film which hung from every portion of the ceiling.

"I had to make three hundred exposures," he said, "and then analyze the results by mathematical computation but everything checked out in the end and all is a success."

Gloriana looked blankly at Tully. "All of what is a success?" Tully asked.

"In one moment I will give you a little demonstration and then I will explain," said the doctor. "That is always the best way. A demonstration first, and then the explanation." He was plainly in the best of humor and enjoying himself. He went to a cupboard and returned carrying a wine bottle, a piece of fishing net and a length of stout rope.

"Strange apparatus, eh?" he said, nodding his head over the three items. "But one can never tell what will provide scientific equipment." Tully examined the wine bottle closely. It was a bottle of Pinot Grand Fenwick, but the cork had been removed and replaced by a metal plug from which a little pipe thrust out, not unlike a pouring device such as is used in serving whisky in bars.

"It was the bobolinks that started it all," said Dr. Kokintz. "But be patient and you will learn everything." To their surprise he then wrapped the fishing net entirely around the wine bottle and tied the rope to the net. The other end of the rope he fastened to the leg of a workbench. Then he stood before the two of them holding the wine bottle upside down in the net, with the rope attached to it.

"In one minute we will start," he said. "We should have a countdown." He glanced at his wrist watch and started counting, "Fifty . . . forty-five . . . forty . . . thirty-five . . ." and then, "ten, nine, eight, seven, six, five, four, three, two, one."

At the word *one* the wine bottle moved a little from side to side in the doctor's hands and then, steadying, rose gracefully up in the air toward the ceiling, accelerating as it went. It was brought to a sudden halt by the rope attached to the fishing net around it. The rope was stretched as stiff as a bar of steel. Tully and Gloriana stared at the wine bottle straining in the air at the top of the rope.

"Whatever is it?" asked Tully, who was the first to recover from his surprise.

"Pinotium Sixty-four," said Dr. Kokintz. "A new element obtained from Pinot Grand Fenwick—Premier Cru." He turned to Gloriana, "Sixty-four is the atomic number," he said. "It also happens to be my age," he added charmingly.

Tully got up and tested the tension of the rope by pulling down on it. He expected it to give, but he could not budge it an inch. He pulled harder without success and finally got his whole weight on the rope, lifting his feet off the floor. The rope remained stiff, the bottle thrust up toward the ceiling did not move by as much as a centimeter. But when Tully, using all his weight on the rope, jerked downward on it, the net around the bottle broke and the bottle itself, with a subdued roar, rushed upward and, being deflected from the upright at its release, thundered out the tall window of Dr. Kokintz' chambers. It was in sight for only a moment, leaving, such was its speed, a vapor trail behind it. Then, lofting over the mountain top, it disappeared into the clouds. They had all run to the window to watch it.

"I'm sorry, Doctor," said Tully as they looked at the little wisp of vapor the rocketing wine bottle had left hanging in the air like a white silk thread.

"It is of no concern," said Kokintz. "You have had the demonstration, but now the explanation. You saw me take a bottle of wine, wrap it in a fishnet, attach a rope to the net and you saw the bottle rise to the ceiling with sufficient force to support the weight of a man. And you ask yourself what provides this force.

"I have given you the answer but in name only— Pinotium Sixty-four, a new radioactive element I have found in Pinot Grand Fenwick—Premier Grand Cru.

"Now comes the difficult part—to explain this element." He seated himself in his chair, filled his big Oompaul pipe and, in the process of filling it, seemed to be arranging his thoughts so as to be able to explain all about Pinotium 64 to these two people who were by no means scientists.

"I will start from the beginning," he said, "and if you do not understand please stop me and question me. It is always important to ask questions. The foolish ones are the ones who do not understand but do not ask questions.

"Well, it began with a bottle of Pinot Grand Fenwick. I was here one night with the Count of Mountjoy and the cork was ejected from a bottle of Pinot Grand Fenwick which was on that table there. Naturally I assumed that Boyle's law of the expansion of gases was in operation— that the heat of the fire had turned some of the alcohol in the wine into a gas and the gas, mixed with the air in the bottle and both seeking to expand, had pushed the cork out of the bottle.

"I had nothing with which to occupy my mind and I began to wonder what exactly was the alcoholic content of Pinot Grand Fenwick and at what temperatures the various components of the wine would be turned into gas and what solid residue would be left.

"It was an experiment for a schoolboy but nonetheless I decided to undertake it. I set up my apparatus and when the Count of Mountjoy had gone, I worked all that night. I obtained from the wine a very small amount of a whitish residue the greatest portion of which I knew would be sugar, while there would be traces of various minerals and salts as well.

"The following morning I went out with Tully to photograph the bobolinks, putting the photographic plates in one pocket of my overcoat together with the residue from the wine which I had in an envelope."

"I remember you asking about the residue," said Tully.

"Yes," said Kokintz. "I wanted to analyze it and I was afraid if I left it, it might be thrown away by Mrs. Plummer when she did the cleaning.

"When I came to develop the plates I found that they were spoiled as if by a light leak. I examined the camera and could find no light leak. Then I examined the plates more thoroughly. And then I came to suspect that this was not a light leak at all but the effect of radioactive particles on the silver emulsion on the photographic plates.

"But where had these radioactive particles come from? I tested everything I had on at the time, my pencils, pieces of paper, a yo-yo I had in my pocket. I was to mend the string for a boy," he added in an aside to Gloriana. "Everything. They all tested negative. And then I found that the radioactive particles were contained in the white residue which I had obtained from the Pinot Grand Fenwick."

"You mean Pinot Grand Fenwick is radioactive?" asked Tully.

"Not all of it," said Kokintz, "only the Premier Grand Cru. That is what perhaps accounts for its excellence. It contains a radioactive element which I have called Pinotium Sixty-four. It has not been isolated before in any other substance.

"I will not delay you with the details of how I isolated Pinotium Sixty-four from the whitish powder which I distilled from the wine. These particulars, which are so fascinating for the scientist, are without any great interest for the layman. What I brought you here to tell you is something of the nature of Pinotium Sixty-four, for it is a remarkable element and in a properly contrived appliance can provide an almost unlimited source of power."

Neither Tully nor Gloriana made any comment on this statement, delivered in a matter-of-fact manner by Kokintz. So when he had made it, he tamped the tobacco in the bowl of his big Oompaul and spent a little while searching for matches with which to relight it, for it had gone out.

"You are aware," continued Kokintz, "that all matter is made up of atoms and that each atom is like a little universe with nuclear particles which move and gyrate around each other in a manner not unlike the planets of our solar system. The glue which holds these atomic particles in the nucleus we loosely call nuclear energy. In the nuclear bomb, some of this energy—a very tiny portion—is released by the dislodging of some of the nuclear particles and the result is a gigantic explosion.

"Science has known for years that if a controlled release of this nuclear energy could be achieved, the world would have a revolutionary power source. Furthermore, science has known for a long time that atoms contain stores of this energy, but so far we have been able to tap only the energy of uranium and heavy hydrogen. And quadium, of course, which was the element I myself isolated and out of which came the quadium bomb."

He went earnestly on, giving a lecture in nuclear physics which eminent physicists would have been glad to listen to, but which was largely lost on Gloriana and her consort. From it they gathered only that Pinotium 64 contained a number of atomic particles which had the surprising quality of being able to change their charge from negative to positive and back again. Thus, when a positively charged particle of Pinotium 64 came into contact with a positively charged particle from another atomic nucleus, the Pinotium particle immediately (and with great politeness) switched its charge to negative. Far from being repelled, then, by the other positive particle, it was attracted to it, crashed into it, and in dislodging it from the nucleus, released a considerable amount of nuclear energy. If, on the other hand, the Pinotium particle were negative, and came into contact with another negative particle, it immediately took on a positive charge resulting again in a tremendous collision and release of energy.

Tully, who had some memories of World War II, came to the conclusion that the Pinotium particles were like Chase-me-Charlie bombs, which ran down their targets on their own volition; and much as he had revered the wine of his native country before, he now held it in even greater awe, and was uneasy about whether, in view of the characteristics which Kokintz had revealed, it might not one day be regarded as a heinous offence to drink a glass of Pinot Grand Fenwick. He kept the thought to himself, however.

"I have called these particular particles Janus particles," said Dr. Kokintz. "They are named after that god of the Romans who faced in two directions at the same time, and who therefore carried a contradiction within himself. It is a contradiction which is the essence of science, which must constantly look backward in order to see clearly forward."

"I understand about changing from positive to negative," said Tully. "But I don't understand why this characteristic makes the Janus particles in Pinotium Sixty-four so important."

"Ah," said Dr. Kokintz, "that is the critical point. With nuclear fission to date we have used neutrons, which bombard the atomic nucleus and are not repulsed by a positive charge. Sometimes they split an atomic nucleus and release energy. Sometimes they are embedded in it without an energy release.

"To get a chain reaction, each such neutron has to release another to continue the bombardment. But the problem of control has always been before us and although it is theoretically possible to obtain a steady release of energy, as a practical matter, the use to date has been largely as an explosive.

"Again, using neutrons, it has been necessary to bombard elements at the lower end of the atomic scale where the particles of the nucleus are not very tightly bound together.

"The tightly bound nuclei in the middle and upper end of the atomic scale we have not been able to split. But the Janus particle, because of its ability to change its charge, can attrack any atomic nucleus. It is no longer necessary to stick to uranium or hydrogen or quadium. I used plain iron filings in the little experiment you just witnessed—two or three iron filings and so small a portion of Pinotium Sixty-four it would not have covered the head of a pin. You saw the result."

"You mean that Pinotium Sixty-four can release atomic energy from any substance?" asked Tully.

"Theoretically yes," replied Kokintz. "In practice I have tried only iron filings, chalk and carbon and a piece of rubber tire."

"Why doesn't it set up a chain reaction and produce an explosion?" asked Gloriana.

"Because the release of the Janus particles from Pinotium Sixty-four is very slow," said Kokintz. "A particle is released, attacks an atomic nucleus and releases some of the energy by displacing some of the particles in the nucleus. Then there is a tiny interval. And then another Janus particle goes to work. There couldn't be a chain reaction because any neutrons released cannot themselves release energy in the substances used, as would be the case with uranium.

"It would be possible to produce an explosion only by using enormous quantities of Pinotium Sixty-four and having it bombard some loosely knit atomic nucleus like uranium." He smiled, and seemed very happy. "It is a pleasure to produce an atomic reaction that cannot destroy the world," he said. "A great pleasure indeed."

Tully Bascomb had a mind which, though by no means brilliant, was certainly practical. He had been close to out of his depth during much of the previous discussion, and he was beginning to arrive only laboriously at a conclusion which would have leapt, brilliant and complete, into the mind of a man like the Count of Mountjoy. He recalled the bottle which had soared upward with sufficient thrust to support his weight. He put that against the background of the astonishing United States loan of $50,000,000 and a prospect presented itself to him so daring that he hesitated to entertain it.

"Dr. Kokintz," he said cautiously, "am I to understand from you that Pinotium Sixty-four provides us with the key to a tremendous source of power?"

"Yes," said Kokintz, "that is so."

"How much power?" Tully asked.

Kokintz shrugged. "An unlimited power."

"As a practical matter," said Tully, "does Pinotium Sixty-four provide us with a source of sufficient power to take a manned rocket to the moon—and back?"

"Certainly," said Kokintz. He reached in his jacket and

pulled out one of his colored pencils. Then he found an envelope and made a calculation on the back of it. "For a rocket of two hundred tons," he said, "all that would be needed would be a hundred pounds of iron filings and a hogshead of wine."

Tully and Gloriana stared at him as if thunderstruck, incapable of saying a word about the tremendously impossible prospect that now lay before them.

IX

Out in the lonely waters of Ascension Island, in late June of that year, the USS *Quest* was keeping a rendezvous with history. The *Quest* had been commissioned as a destroyer but she was a destroyer with a difference. The difference consisted in the scrapping of all her armament to be replaced by extensive radar equipment, telemetry equipment and other elaborate devices for tracking space capsules on their re-entry into the earth's atmosphere.

The *Quest* was a floating brain, specializing in mathematics by electronics, and was the first ship of her kind to sail the waters of the world. Resting on the surface of one ocean of liquid, she probed into and explored another ocean of air, thrusting her invisible feelers up and around and about into the earth's atmosphere, feeling for her prey which was, as has been said, space capsules making a re-entry.

So sensitive was her equipment that she could pick up several thousand miles away a returning capsule whose telemetry system had failed so that the capsule was not emitting any signal from which its course could be predicted. There was on the USS *Quest* a cunning piece of apparatus called, in keeping with the American penchant for nicknames, "Hotfoot."

Hotfoot was so sensitive to heat changes that it could accurately detect the dramatic rise in temperature of the outer metal of a space capsule as it hit the earth's atmosphere. This information was fed by Hotfoot into an electronic brain which immediately calculated the capsule's position and course, and Hotfoot alone had been responsible for the recovery of many capsules whose own signaling systems had failed and which would otherwise have been lost in the oceans of the world.

The present mission of *Quest* was to pinpoint a very important space capsule. Launched without fanfare from Cape Canaveral in a Saturn rocket fueled with liquid hydrogen, this capsule had been orbited fifty times around the earth. The term *capsule*, though the one in common use, was hardly adequate to describe the present device, which was actually the pilot model of a space platform which would one day—perhaps in so short a time as two years—be put into orbit around the moon as a tremendously important step toward a lunar landing by the United States.

Plainly then it was of the utmost importance that this particular capsule be recovered with the greatest dispatch. The plan was to bring the capsule down in the ocean off Ascension Island and the USS *Quest* was but part of a fleet of ships cruising the area while above flew an armada of planes patrolling the atmosphere to aid in the recovery.

Aboard the *Quest* were Senator John Ridgeway of the Senate Atomic Energy Commission, and Dr. Fritz Meidel, the top atomic physicist responsible for the present project. Dr. Meidel (part of the war booty the United States had obtained following the defeat of Nazi Germany) was at pains to explain to the Senator the talents of the apparatus known as Hotfoot. To give the Senator a practical demonstration, arrangements had been made for one of the planes, invisible some miles above the earth, to drop a few objects down on the ocean.

"You understand, of course, Senator," said Dr. Meidel, "that whatever is dropped from the plane for Hotfoot to locate, will come down only under the force of gravity. The temperature change in this object then will be extremely slight. And yet this device will be able to record it, and locate the object."

"What causes this temperature change anyway?" asked the Senator.

"Collision with the particles of which the atmosphere is composed," replied Dr. Meidel. "Any object moving through the air at speed, comes into collision with the molecules of oxygen, hydrogen and so on, and these hitting against it produce a temperature change which is related to the speed of the object."

Anxious to make things as plain as possible to the Senator and conscious that what he had said smacked slightly of the lecture hall, Dr. Meidel added, "It's the same thing as beating on a piece of iron with a hammer. If you beat on a piece of iron with a hammer for a while, you will find that the iron gets a little hotter."

"That so?" said the Senator. "Can't say I ever tried it."

They were in the control room of Hotfoot, before them a glass screen about the size of that of a large television set. The operator, busy with some dials and switches, said suddenly, "Here's something now, sir. Sixty thousand feet, course a hundred and sixty. It will hit the water four thousand yards to the southwest of us." He gestured to the screen on which a few droplets of light indicated the course of whatever had been jettisoned by a plane overhead for the Senator's edification.

"Could we pick it up when it hits?" asked the Senator. "I'd like to take something home to the kid as a souvenir."

"I'm afraid not, Senator," said Dr. Meidel. "It would have sunk by the time we got there."

"What do you suppose it is?" asked the Senator.

"Probably a small sandbag," replied the scientist.

"Here's another, sir," said the operator. He was a bright young man, had heard the Senator's remark about a souvenir and he was in luck. "It's going to land much nearer to us. About a hundred feet off our port bow. If you step outside right away you may see it when it hits the water."

The Senator rushed outside followed by Dr. Meidel. They looked up into the sky and saw a tiny flash hurtling toward them as swift as a kingfisher. It plummeted suddenly into the ocean, the impact marked by a sharp flick of white spume spouting up from the lovely blue. A few seconds later something could be seen floating in the water where the object had struck.

"It didn't sink," cried the Senator. "That's near enough to pick up, isn't it?" he demanded. "My kid would sure like to get it."

Dr. Meidel nodded and spoke to one of the ship's officers, and without any delay a boat was launched and made for the spot. The boat returned, the cox'n carrying the object which had been picked out of the sea. He was about to give it to Dr. Meidel but the doctor was at that moment called into the Hotfoot control room and the Senator grabbed the object and held it up in some surprise.

"Well, what do you know?" he said. "A wine bottle." He looked from the bottle up in the air and then, turning to one of the ship's officers, said with mock severity, "Aren't there some kind of regulations about taking intoxicating drinks up in United States airplanes?"

"I'm sure the bottle was empty, sir," said the officer to whom the question was addressed.

"It's empty now anyway," said the Senator. "Look, it's got a kind of thing in the end for pouring." He looked the bottle over, "Pinot Grand Fenwick— Premier Grand Cru," he read aloud from the label. "Never heard of it," he announced, "but I guess Butchie will be glad to have it."

The others smiled and the Senator went down to his quarters with the bottle.

Meanwhile Grand Fenwick went seriously into the project of sending a rocket to the moon. The tiny country had, in one dramatic breakthrough, actually leapt ahead of both the United States and the Soviet Union. These two giants were still bedeviled by the problem of developing an ideal rocket fuel. Using iron filings and wine—both extremely cheap ingredients, though one shrinks at the use of the word "cheap" in connection with so noble a vintage as Pinot Grand Fenwick—the little Duchy had discovered an atomic fuel which, not requiring oxygen in any form for combustion, was the perfect answer for travel in the voids of space.

Grand Fenwick was further not handicapped by a desire to amass a huge quantity of scientific data during the lunar trip. There was to be no study of radiation in outer space, of the incidence of meteorites (some of them no bigger than a grain of dust) or of exterior temperatures compared with interior temperatures of the rocket, nor of all the other facets of space travel with which both the United States and the Soviet Union were concerned.

In short the Duchy aimed at no more than getting to the moon, landing on it, and getting back again, and this enormously reduced the amount of work necessary in designing the rocket while at the same time cutting down on the payload of instruments and providing larger and more comfortable quarters for the Grand Fenwick astronauts.

To be sure, there was a political problem in Grand Fenwick which lay in Mountjoy's attempt to use the money on bathtubs rather than on rockets. But when Tully Bascomb announced to a meeting of the Council of Freemen that in Pinotium 64, Grand Fenwick had the fuel needed to send a rocket to the moon, Mountjoy hadn't got a chance. What had previously been a fantastic proposal, was now well within the reach of the country. Excitement over the project rose to fever pitch among the people and remained at that level. Nothing else was talked about and all the men of the Duchy volunteered their services to help in whatever manner they could.

Mountjoy made one gallant but impossible stand. "Are we," he demanded of the Council, "to allow our great wine to be converted into a kind of gasoline for fueling space vehicles? For that is the prospect which now lies before you. Pinot Grand Fenwick has been revered by connoisseurs of wine for five hundred years. It is the superior wine of the world, without question.

"You are all aware that the great Queen Isabella of Spain gave a bottle to Columbus when he set out on his first voyage of discovery, telling him that if at any point in his venture he should lose heart, one sip would restore his courage.

"You are aware that when Columbus faced a mutiny among his men, he opened that bottle of Pinot Grand Fenwick and, giving a little to each member of his crew, staved off a mutiny which would have resulted in the failure of that expedition which opened the whole of the New World to Europe.

"Such has been the stature of Pinot Grand Fenwick through the years. Gentlemen, are you now going to turn this noble product into a kind of superior petrol—available, one presumes, at gasoline pumps throughout the world wherever anyone wishes to take off in a rocket?"

But the Count hadn't got a hope. Bentner followed him with an accusation that the Count of Mountjoy, as usual, was opposing the interests of the rocket fuel, then this provided an additional market for the primary product of the Duchy and this would benefit the workers whose representative he was. There was nothing whatever to stop people from continuing to drink Pinot Grand Fenwick and he foresaw an even greater demand for it, for people needing ten gallons for their cars (he foresaw cars driven by rocket engines) would not neglect to also drink a glass themselves. No other gasoline embodied such an appeal, doing good for man and motor. Bentner sat down amidst thunderous applause and Mountjoy, realizing that he was defeated, accepted the situation and concentrated on ensuring that he got five million for his plumbing. A few days later he had wisely altered his stand, completely reversed his position "out of deference to the expressed ideas of the people" and was as firm a promoter of the rocket project as anyone in the Duchy.

"A great statesman is always at the service of the people," he told his son Vincent smoothly. "Particularly if to oppose the people is to forfeit his position. No figure is so pathetic as the discredited leader who had not the wisdom to swing with the tide. History has little place for him, and he becomes the subject of research by students desperate for a thesis with which to win a degree. And that, my boy, is the limbo of those whose lack of discretion costs them immortality."

Vincent grunted. He had learned to accept these lessons in statesmanship from his father without comment. He had been put in charge of the actual construction of the rocket, subject to Dr. Kokintz, as the master architect, and although nothing was said immediately, it was understood that these would be the two who would man the rocket at its take-off.

Vincent's first job was to find a launching site. He considered for a while launching the rocket from a plain concrete pad in the open, and this could certainly have been done. But Grand Fenwick's weather was not a match for Florida's. Many days the rain and wind would hold up work and provide problems of deterioration of the metal casing of the rocket. It would be better to work under cover, and surveying the castle one day with his father (incidental to installing plumbing, which he had also agreed to do) he fell to examining the large tower on the northeast corner of the castle. It was called the Jericho Tower, since its base was adjacent to the Jericho room of the castle, so named because it contained a large stained-glass window depicting the fall of the Walls of Jericho.

"What's in that?" he asked of his father, the Count.

"The remnants of a spiral staircase—one of the largest in Europe," Mountjoy replied. "It has not been used since fifteen eighty-seven."

"Why?" asked Vincent, studying the tall, slim but strong lines of the tower.

"In that year the Spanish ambassador, coming down the stairs ahead of the English ambassador, fell, rolled to the bottom and was killed. The Spanish maintained that their ambassador had been pushed by the Englishman. Grand Fenwick arbitrated the matter, deciding that it was an accident, but Spain seized on the incident anyway and sent her Armada against England—with disastrous results. They would have been far better off to have taken our decision in the first place."

"I thought England's war with Spain resulted from England's raids on Spanish possessions in the New World," said Vincent absently, for he was still studying the tower.

"That is merely the English version," said the Count of Mountjoy. "The interpretation of history largely depends on the nationality of the nation in which it is published." The two went into the tower and Vincent inspected the masonry carefully. He found it in excellent shape. The circular staircase on the interior could be removed without impairing the structural strength.

"By golly, I think it is just what we need!" exclaimed Vincent.

"Need for what?" asked his father.

"Need for the rocket. We can assemble the rocket in the

bottom of the tower, which connects with the dungeons of the castle—providing an excellent sheltered working area—and launch the rocket through the top of the tower."

"From the Tower of Jericho?" demanded the Count.

"Certainly," said Vincent. "Why not?"

The Count thought it over for a moment. "Why not indeed?" he said, smiling. "I think in view of the likely effect that it would be most appropriate."

And so, a building and launching site having been decided upon, the work went on and Grand Fenwick made no attempt to keep secret the building of its rocket. Yet the fact that the work had been put in hand was not credited for a moment by the United States, Russia or any other country. But that was not the Duchy's fault.

The Count of Mountjoy paid a special visit to the United States Ambassador in Switzerland (who handled American affairs in the Duchy but never visited it as being too small and inaccessible a place) to tell him that the Duchy was building a rocket to send to the moon. The Ambassador, who was, of course, aware of the loan the United States had made to Grand Fenwick for this purpose, nodded politely and asked from where the rocket would be launched.

"From the Tower of Jericho," replied the Count of Mountjoy, quite seriously, at which the Ambassador smiled and said he thought that highly appropriate. He made no official report on this visit but passed the story on through diplomatic circles so that it became a well-known anecdote, not given the slightest credence anywhere.

In selecting the Tower of Jericho at the castle as the launching silo, Grand Fenwick had taken an important but unwitting step toward keeping its rocket project a secret. Soon the story was so well known that any utterly implausible project was referred to as a "Tower of Jericho." After that it would have been extremely difficult, without a tremendous effort, to get anyone to believe seriously in the Grand Fenwick lunar rocket. Perhaps if matters had gone differently from the start, the world would not have remained for so long in ignorance. But circumstances conspired to prevent the story being believed—circumstances and the intensive propaganda of the Union of Soviet Socialist Republics, working as hard as it could to offset the effect of America's gift of $50,000,000 as a practical step toward international co-operation in the conquest of the moon.

Had there been any analysis of the orders placed in the United States by Grand Fenwick, utilizing the $50,000,000 given the Duchy, a clue to what was going on in Grand Fenwick might have been discovered. But these orders went to the United States government purchasing agency which agreed to buy on behalf of Grand Fenwick and they were filled without any investigation whatever.

Copies of the orders went, of course, to the desk of Frederick Paxton Wendover in charge of the Central European Desk in the State Department for his routine information. He hardly had time to give them more than a glance. In any case, most of them seemed to deal with piping, heaters, bathtubs, shower stalls, shower heads, and other items connected with plumbing; and as he pointed out to the Secretary of State, his analysis of the situation had been correct. What Grand Fenwick was really after was modern plumbing. He was surprised, however, one day to get a call from the government purchasing agency referring him to one order from Grand Fenwick requisitioning a discarded Saturn rocket casing.

"What the hell am I supposed to do about this?" asked the purchasing-agency man. "We don't sell used rockets to foreign powers. What do they want it for anyway?"

"Hanged if I know," said Wendover. "I'll call you back."

He turned to his copy of the order and read it over. The requisition asked for forty oversized bathtubs, a large quantity of turquoise glazed tiling, several thousand feet of copper piping in various sizes and then, "One used Saturn rocket, without engine or instrumentation." He was shocked and thought about it for a while and then smiled.

"Astute old fox," he said to himself, thinking of Mountjoy. "He is well aware of the Russian efforts to discredit the sincerity of our loan and hopes to help us out by ordering a Saturn rocket shell. Well, we ought to give him one. We can circulate the word that we are supplying it and that will put the Russians on the spot again. They can't continue with their present line that the money was just an empty gesture and is being spent on bathtubs. Mountjoy will probably convert it into a water heater, though. He'd need something of that size in that castle."

He called the National Space Agency and rather surprised them by asking if they had a used Saturn rocket available. It turned out they had several whose shells had failed metallurgical tests, being a few millimeters out of true—an important factor in avoiding heat buildup at tremendous speeds.

"Frankly we don't know what to do with them," said the man at the Space Agency. "They're an embarrassment to us. We can't throw them in a junkyard because there'd be a national outcry. If we start cutting them up there'd be hell to pay too. And we haven't got storage space for them. We offered them to a few cities around the nation for erection in parks as monuments or something, but no cities want to pay the cost of moving them and we haven't any funds for that purpose. So they're just racked up and we're beginning to run out of space."

"What are they worth?" asked Wendover.

"Worth? Well, they cost several million bucks apiece. That's what they cost. But they're not *worth* anything."

"Are you prepared to part with one if the customer will pay the cost of transport?" asked Wendover.

"Sure," said the Space Agency man. "Who's the customer, by the way?"

"The Duchy of Grand Fenwick."

"Oh yeah. The Tower of Jericho boys," and he chuckled and hung up.

Wendover called back the purchasing agency and told them where they could get a used Saturn rocket and told them to go ahead and supply it. He then informed the Secretary of State, who also thought that it was pretty nice of the Count of Mountjoy to back the United States up in this manner.

"And then people say we haven't any real friends in Europe," he said. "Well, they're wrong. The Duchy of Grand Fenwick is solidly behind us."

He mentioned the incident to the President, who was touched by the loyalty and thoughtfulness of Grand Fenwick in ordering the used rocket. A statement was issued to the press regarding the purchase and the story was dutifully printed and broadcast. But the editors chuckled as they sent it through to the printers for setting and the readers chuckled when they read it in their newspapers because everybody knew that a country as small as Grand Fenwick couldn't be serious about sending a rocket to the moon.

Everybody, that is, but Grand Fenwick. There, under Vincent of Mountjoy's direction, they just went ahead building the rocket in the Tower of Jericho.

X

Amidst all the strenuous activity of preparing the Grand Fenwick rocket for launching, Dr. Kokintz still had time to keep up a vigorous correspondence with the Audubon Society and with bird lovers in many parts of the world on the subject of the two bobolinks which had taken up their residence in the forest of Grand Fenwick. He had sent to the society his pictures of the two birds, native to the northeastern coast of America, which had appeared in the Duchy; and the publication of these pictures in the journal of the society created a tremendous sensation.

A furor of speculation was immediately aroused over how the birds got to the Duchy, so far from their native habitat. It was well known to bird lovers that bobolinks migrate during the winter months to South America by way of the West Indies, but there was no case on record of a migration to Europe. A theory was advanced that a party of bobolinks, headed northward for New England and Southern Canada, had been swept off their course by a hurricane off the Florida coast, the survivors reaching Europe, and the Grand Fenwick bobolinks were of this party.

A hunt among bird watchers for other bobolinks in Europe was immediately instigated, but without conclusive results. One was reported in Sicily and three in the South of France, but no photographs were available. Then a rumor started that the whole thing was a hoax and that the Kokintz photographs had been taken not in Grand Fenwick but in the woodlands of Connecticut.

Kokintz was horrified by this suggestion. He was a simple man, almost childish; used to believing others and to being believed himself. He protested strongly against the hoax story and invited anyone who was interested to come to Grand Fenwick and see the bobolinks for themselves.

One day he received a letter from Bern, Switzerland, from a certain Mr. Maurice Spender. Mr. Spender said that he was an Englishman and a keen ornithologist and that he was prepared to produce letters from the highest authorities attesting to his lifelong interest in birds. He asked whether he might be permitted to come to Grand Fenwick and see the two bobolinks for himself, and take photographs of them.

"Why all the fuss about letters of recommendation?" asked Tully when Kokintz showed him this letter. "Anyone who wants is welcome to come here and see the bobolinks."

Kokintz shrugged. "It is the British," he said. "They are a very formal people. They have a horror of pretenders and like to have everything certified and authenticated. England is the only country in the world where it is a serious offense to wear the wrong tie, because it puts you in the position of masquerading as something you are not."

Tully nodded. "Write and tell him to come by all means," he said. "We can put him up at the castle. If he were coming a couple of months from now, we could even give him a hot bath. He might like to see the rocket while he is here."

Dr. Kokintz did not think so. "A real bird lover," he said, "would not be interested in things like rockets." He produced a small clipping from a newspaper which had been enclosed with Mr. Spender's letter. It was a communication to the editor of *The Times* in London and read:

Sir:
At 6:15 this morning, I distinctly heard the notes of a cuckoo in a small spinney near my house. The call was repeated for four minutes and then ceased. Is this the first cuckoo to be heard in Hampshire this year?

Maurice Spender

Alston,
Hampshire,
March 3, 1966.

"Note the date on that," said Dr. Kokintz.
"What about the date?" asked Tully.
"Well, just the day before, the world was staggered by the announcement that the United States had managed to put a satellite in orbit around the planet Venus. But Mr. Spender did not care about the satellite. He was out listening for the first cuckoo of spring. That is a bird watcher for you." Dr. Kokintz seemed immensely pleased with Mr. Spender.

The doctor indeed looked forward eagerly to the arrival of Mr. Spender, and met him personally at the Swiss frontier of Grand Fenwick, where Mr. Spender got off the bus a week later. He had with him not one camera but several, all of expensive makes and all of them new. He also had a fishing rod and a double-barreled shotgun and several pieces of luggage. He was dressed in very hairy tweeds, the trousers seeming somewhat large for him. The tweeds were of a rust-red and beneath the jacket he had a pullover of bright yellow.

"Dr. Kokintz?" he said, extending his hand vigorously. "Jolly nice of you to meet me. Been looking forward to this immensely. Can't wait until I see your bobobinks."

"Bobolinks," said Kokintz.

"Of course, bobolinks," said Spender. "Silly slip of the tongue. Ride on that bus upset me. You haven't got a car, I see. Can we get a taxi?"

Kokintz explained that there were no automobiles at all in Grand Fenwick, but they could leave Mr. Spender's luggage where it was by the side of the road and send a cart for it from the castle. But Mr. Spender was not prepared to leave his gear unguarded. He said it contained many things of value and he would be very distressed if anything were missing.

"Nobody will touch it," Kokintz assured him. "It will be perfectly safe here. Nobody steals anything in Grand Fenwick." But Mr. Spender was not to be persuaded and Dr. Kokintz had to go off for a cart himself. When he returned,

Mr. Spender was not to be found immediately. He was located, looking rather sheepish, in the top branches of a large sycamore, from which vantage point he seemed to have been taking pictures of Fenwick castle with a telescopic lens.

"Wonderful view of the castle from up there," he said, climbing down from the tree.

"There's a much better view around the corner of the road," said Dr. Kokintz.

"I wanted to frame it in the top branches of the tree," said Mr. Spender. "Something different, you know." But the explanation, in view of the work involved in climbing to the top of the tree and down again, sounded lame.

"He's a real Englishman," Dr. Kokintz said to himself. "Eccentric like they all are." He recalled that during his student days a fellow student from England had tried to cure himself of influenza by sleeping out in subzero weather. His theory was that influenza germs could not survive severe cold. He caught double pneumonia and died.

Mr. Spender found a welcoming committee waiting for him at the Castle of Grand Fenwick. On hand were Gloriana, Tully, the Count of Mountjoy, his son Vincent and, of course, David Bentner representing the workingman.

They all went off to breakfast, whose preparation the Duchess herself had supervised out of fondness for Dr. Kokintz. It was a very English breakfast, bacon, eggs, kidneys and cold toast. Gloriana had wanted the toast hot, but Tully, who was much more traveled than she, said the English always ate cold toast for breakfast and, to ensure that it was cold, put it in a thing called a toast rack where it had maximum exposure to the air and so could lose all its heat before being eaten. The talk during the breakfast was rather awkward. Spender was not much of a conversationalist, or perhaps the bus ride from Bern had deprived him of the use of his wits. Mountjoy remarked that he had brought a rod with him, and Spender said briskly that he hoped to get in a little fishing.

"What had you in mind?" asked Mountjoy.

"Trout," said Spender.

"Trout?" cried Mountjoy. "But the May fly aren't on the river yet."

"Actually I'm not much of a fisherman," said Mr. Spender. "I only bought the rod the other day. Thought it might be nice to do a little fishing while bird watching."

Kokintz agreed kindly that that seemed like a good idea and turned the conversation to birds. "I have counted a hundred and twenty-five species in our forests in the course of one month," he said. "A wonderful variety for so small an area. There have been eight kinds of tits alone in one day and last year by the river we found a pair of kingfishers. It is unusual, as you know, to find them at any altitude. They normally prefer the lower reaches of rivers." He went on about birds and Spender told them about the time he had heard the cuckoo in Hampshire on March 3 at 6:15 A.M. and asked Dr. Kokintz if he could have the clipping from *The Times* back as it was the only one he had and he treasured it. The doctor promised to return it to him. Spender seemed to recall something and reached into his inner pocket and produced an envelope.

"My credentials," he said and gave the envelope to Dr. Kokintz. It contained a number of letters from various consular officials, all in Switzerland, attesting that Mr. Spender was a bird watcher.

These were circulated around the table, read politely, and handed back to Mr. Spender.

"Really," said Dr. Kokintz, "it wasn't necessary for you to go to the trouble to get all that accreditation. We are quite prepared to accept you as a bird watcher if that is what you say you are."

"In my business," said Mr. Spender, "I like to be able to produce the proper credentials. I regard that as important."

"I'm afraid you will just have to take *us* at our word," said Gloriana. "None of us has any papers to say who we are."

"That is quite a different matter," said Mr. Spender. "Quite a different matter. You don't need papers. I do." He gave them all a bright smile and stuffed the envelope back in his pocket.

"While you're here," said Vincent of Mountjoy, "I wonder whether you wouldn't like to look over our rocket?"

"Rocket?" said Mr. Spender and he looked very surprised.

"Yes," said Vincent. "We are preparing to send one to the moon. Should be ready in a few weeks now. Dr. Kokintz and I are going in it."

A look of deep caution came over Mr. Spender's face. "Ah, of course," he said, "of course," repeating the two words as if they conveyed a deep but secret significance which was nonetheless known to all present.

Vincent, who was very keen on the rocket, was puzzled by the caution displayed but plunged enthusiastically on. "We were able to obtain a Saturn rocket casing from the United States for nothing more than the cost of transportation," he said. "We got it in pieces and put it together in the dungeon and it is installed in the Jericho Tower. The whole thing is in its most interesting stage of construction right now and I would be delighted to take you on a tour of it."

"I really came to see the bobobinks," said Mr. Spender. "I cannot pretend to be greatly interested in the rocket."

"Oh, you can't leave Grand Fenwick without seeing it," said Vincent. "Why don't you let me take you around, and then this evening you can see the bobolinks. It's better to see them in the evening, isn't it, Doctor?"

"Dawn or sunset. Those are the best times," said Dr. Kokintz. "For birds and worms," he added.

"Well," said Mr. Spender, "if you wish. Certainly people would be likely to ask me about it, wouldn't they?" But he didn't really seem very keen, and when, after breakfast, Vincent led him down the spiral staircase to the dungeon, he brought only one of his poorer cameras with him with a cheap flashgun attachment.

Vincent was annoyed that Mr. Spender should not think his rocket worth an expensive camera, but, glad to explain the ingenuity he had exercised in the construction of the rocket, was soon lost in explaining its details.

The interior had been laid out in three sections. The one nearest the nose was to be the living quarters of the two astronauts. It was to contain bunks, a table, chairs and several periscopes out of which the astronauts could peer to obtain a panoramic view around their space ship. The floor was of steel but with a number of circular holes through it. "Sort of a shock absorber," said Vincent. "To combat the initial acceleration when we take off. It's liable to be pretty rough. The carpet will also reduce vibration and make it easier for us to hear each other."

Mr. Spender nodded but didn't seem to believe this and was, in fact, not very interested in any part of the rocket; even when Vincent showed him the air jets, which would meter oxygen into the compartment for the astronauts, and the air-conditioning system, which removed all the air in the compartment every few hours, making it flow over chemicals which would remove the carbon dioxide.

"I got the idea both from the work done in submarines since the Second World War and also closed-circuit diving systems which use the same principle," Vincent explained. "As you know, atomic submarines have to stay down for a long time with a large crew and no access to fresh air. They use something of the same system as I have installed here."

Mr. Spender took one picture of the interior of the compartment, but Vincent got the impression that he was doing it out of politeness. He next showed his visitor the second compartment below, which contained the needed stores for the trip. But again Mr. Spender was not much interested and complained of feeling hot. The third and bottom compartment contained the engine of the rocket.

"A completely new fuel source," said Vincent, sure that this would arouse Mr. Spender's interest. "An atomic fuel, in fact. This will be the world's first atomic rocket." At this Mr. Spender picked up his ears.

"Atomic-powered?" he asked, and his surprise was genuine.

"Yes," said Vincent. "That is Dr. Kokintz' great discovery. He has isolated an element, Pinotium Sixty-four containing a curious particle called the Janus particle, which can change its charge from positive to negative. It is the Janus particle that provides the key to the whole thing." Vincent explained about the Janus particle and Mr. Spender listened very carefully.

"And where does this Pinotium Sixty-four come from?" he asked.

"From wine. . . . Pinot Grand Fenwick, Premier Grand Cru," said Vincent.

Mr. Spender gave Vincent a pleasant look as if to indicate that he thought Vincent was an idiot but was intent on humoring him. "From wine," he said. "Of course. From wine."

"Wouldn't you like to take a photograph of the jet clusters?" asked Vincent. "I had quite a problem with them. I couldn't think of a system of directing the jets in any desired direction to maneuver the rocket. And then I found a real fancy shower head my father had ordered from America— you know he's installing modern plumbing in the castle—and it was just the thing. It will spray water in a solid stream, in jets like from the nozzle of a watering can, or sort of reverse itself, throwing water up in the air instead of downward. I think that feature was designed for people in America who like to take a shower but have tender heads. Anyway, that's what we're using as jets on the rocket."

"Shower heads?" asked Mr. Spender incredulously.

"Yes," said Vincent. "They work fine. Of course, Father was a bit angry because he wanted these shower heads for the bathrooms. But he agreed to let me have them since the rocket came first and he's ordered another shipment from America for the castle."

He pointed below the rocket to where a number of gleaming chrome shower heads were fastened to the bottom of the rocket by stout steel brackets. A network of steel piping connected the shower heads with the interior of the rocket and Vincent said they led to the reaction chamber.

"Want to take a picture?" Vincent asked.

"No," said Mr. Spender firmly. "I think not."

The tour of the rocket concluded, Vincent led Mr. Spender across the floor of the dungeon to the exit. On their way they passed several racks of copper piping stacked against the dungeon wall. A group of workmen had taken away some of the masonry of the wall and were inserting some of the piping through it. Several sections of a massive furnace stood nearby.

"What's all that?" asked Mr. Spender, stopping by the copper pipes.

"Oh nothing," said Vincent, now somewhat irritated with him. "It's just part of the piping for the castle plumbing."

"Is that so?" asked Mr. Spender. "Do you mind if I take a picture?"

"It's only plumbing," said Vincent, miffed that his rocket had been given such scant shrift. "I don't know what you would want to take a picture of it for."

"Nonetheless it is interesting," said Mr. Spender, and he leveled his camera and shot a flash photo of the racks of copper pipe.

"Another one is permitted?" asked Mr. Spender.

"Oh come on," said Vincent, thoroughly fed up. "Dr. Kokintz is probably waiting for you." But Mr. Spender nonetheless shot a picture of the parts of the furnace lying about and then, and only reluctantly, followed Vincent out of the dungeon. Dr. Kokintz proposed that they might go that evening to get a picture of the bobolinks, but Mr. Spender said that he was rather tired from his traveling and the following evening might be better.

He retired to his apartment, which was close to that of the Count of Mountjoy. Gloriana politely inquired whether he would like to have dinner in his room if he wished to rest. To this Mr. Spender agreed and he was not seen about the castle for the rest of the day.

"Bird watching is a fatiguing business," said Dr. Kokintz at dinner that evening, for he was a firm ally of Mr. Spender's. "I have no doubt he has been up many, many times at dawn and is in need of a good rest."

"What did you think of him, Vincent?" asked Gloriana.

"He's a queer duck," said Vincent. "Shot one picture of the rocket and two of the plumbing. Why do you suppose he would want to take a picture of some workmen putting copper piping in the walls of a fourteenth-century castle?" he asked of his father.

"Ah, my boy," said the Count of Mountjoy, "there you have an interesting comment on the English character—to which I might add our own character is somewhat related, for let us never forget that Grand Fenwick was founded by Englishmen.

"Many of the English nobility live in castles like these and have been freezing in them for years, lacking every kind of convenience but so bound by tradition that they will do nothing to modernize them. Modern piping being run through the walls of a fourteenth-century castle would be much more interesting to an Englishman than a rocket designed to go to the moon. He'll show those pictures around his club time and time again, and always to an incredulous audience. I still think that the modernizing of this castle will in the long run redound more to the credit of Grand Fenwick than the success of that rocket you are working on. To get to the moon and back is undoubtedly an astounding feat. But to be able to have a hot bath whenever one wants it—that is an enduring contribution to the refinement of man, which is the proper objective of all governments."

"Bobo," said Gloriana, "you are not running for re-election at the present moment."

"What is your estimate now on the take-off date for the rocket?" asked Tully, turning to Vincent of Mountjoy.

"Four weeks," said Vincent. "But that's just the engineering end of it. Dr. Kokintz will have to set the time because he has to calculate the orbit."

"The twentieth of July would be the best date," said Dr. Kokintz. "At that time the moon will be at its perigee." He looked apologetically at Gloriana, for he always felt self-conscious about using terms that others might not understand, though now and again one slipped out. "I mean that the moon will be closest to earth at that time and the distance between the two will be about twenty-six thousand miles less than when the moon is at its farthest from the earth."

"You speak about it all in such a casual way," said Gloriana. "It is still difficult for me to believe that all this is going to take place."

"It isn't really such a big event," said Kokintz. "From the surface of the earth to the surface of the moon when the two are closest together is only about two hundred and twenty thousand miles in round figures. Very many people travel such a distance these days in the course of their lives, though not all at once. The distance then is a trifle. What makes the project seem so dramatic is leaving earth to venture into space to the moon. But the moon is really a part of earth, though we haven't visited it before. It is the little sister of earth. We should not be so astounded at traveling the small distance that separates the two. Men have done much more remarkable things than that."

"For example?" asked Gloriana.

"Well," said Dr. Kokintz, "learning to write. The ability to transfer the intangible thoughts in one man's mind to another man's mind by the use of a series of symbols called letters—that is much more remarkable than going to the moon. But it is so commonplace that it does not seem remarkable to us. When we have got used to making lunar trips, we will all be surprised that so much fuss was made about the first one."

"You are so sure you will be able to get there—and return?" asked Gloriana.

"We will be back for Your Grace's birthday celebration," said Kokintz. "And if we find any rare stone on the moon, we will bring it back for you as a birthday gift."

"Just bring back yourselves," said Gloriana softly. "That is all I could desire."

"I think that by then the bobolinks will have a nest full of fledglings," said Kokintz to Tully.

"Yes," said Tully. "I think so." But at this point the conversation lagged and they all fell quiet, thinking of the twentieth of July—a date which now overshadowed all the others on the calendar, as if it were the date of Doomsday.

XI

Later that same evening Vincent of Mountjoy called on Cynthia Bentner and the two went for a walk together down the road which skirted the Forest of Grand Fenwick. Vincent, busy with the rocket for the past several weeks, had not seen much of Cynthia for he had had on many occasions to work far into the night. He felt a strong need for her company now, but, as they walked together, had so little to say that Cynthia wondered whether she had in some way offended him.

"Have I done anything wrong?" she asked after a while.

"No," said Vincent. "I just don't feel much like talking. I want to be with you but my mind keeps returning to the rocket and the journey to the moon. Gloriana said at dinner this evening that she could hardly bring herself to realize that the whole project was true, and ever since I started working on it, I've had the feeling of being in a dream, and wouldn't be very surprised if I woke up and discovered that, after all, it *was* only a dream."

"It's not a dream for me," said Cynthia, "but a nightmare. I wish I could wake up and find that it was all nothing but my imagination, and there wasn't any rocket. And yet if there wasn't a rocket you would be leaving Grand Fenwick and going perhaps to America and I wouldn't see you again."

"Please don't say that," said Vincent.

"What?" said Cynthia.

"Don't ever say anything about not seeing me again. It isn't that I'm afraid of what might happen. But just the thought of not seeing you again—well, that frightens me. I don't mind dying as dying. But since dying would entail not seeing you again—then I am afraid of it."

"You never spoke like this to me before," said Cynthia.

"I wasn't able to get anything into focus before," replied Vincent. "It's hard to explain how it was with me. I hated Grand Fenwick. I didn't want to be here. It was like being buried alive. I couldn't use my mind or my training here. And yet the thought of going to someplace where I could do useful work, but being without you, was more than I could bring myself to face. I was almost content to be buried alive—well, not content, but resigned to it. And yet I knew that wouldn't work. I couldn't cut myself off from my future to be here with you."

"I could go with you wherever you wanted to go," said Cynthia quietly.

Vincent shook his head. "That wouldn't do," he said. "You have a kind of a goodness to you that would just get you hurt over and over again anywhere but here. You are like the earth—you are strong and enduring and peaceful and goodness grows out of you."

"If I'm like that," said Cynthia, "nothing would change me wherever I was."

"In the cities," said Vincent, "they take the earth and pour cement over it and put buildings up on top and it isn't the earth any longer. It dies."

"I planned to get that money spent on the rocket, during the election, so that there would be something to keep you here with me," said Cynthia. "But what was I to do? If there wasn't the rocket to keep you here, you would have gone. And now the rocket means that you will go anyway —much farther away than New York or London; to a place no living creature has ever been before. Oh Vincent, I'm terrified that you won't be able to get back."

He took her in his arms and held her tightly. "I will get back," he said. "I will get back. There will be you to bring me back here and that will be enough. Besides," he added cheerfully, "there's absolutely nothing that can go wrong with the rocket. It's foolproof. It's the engineer's ideal—a machine which functions without moving parts. The nuclear stream thrusts out of the jets in the back and the rocket takes off. That's all. And it is much easier to get from the moon to the earth than from the earth to the moon, because the moon's gravitational pull is only one-sixth of that of earth. That means that to take off from the moon, we need only one-sixth of the power required to take off from here."

He talked enthusiastically about the rocket, explained the method by which it would reverse itself when landing on the moon, coming down on legs which would be extended from it at the right time. "It will land so gently," he said, "that it will be just like a fly landing on a table top. Much the worst part of the whole trip will be the take-off from here because of the huge acceleration we have to develop to escape from the gravitational pull of the earth. The power requirement decreases as we get farther and farther away."

"How long will it take?" asked Cynthia.

"Nine days and four hours," said Vincent.

"So long?" asked Cynthia. "I thought it would be much quicker than that."

"We're only going to go at a thousand miles an hour," said Vincent. "It's Dr. Kokintz' idea and I thoroughly agree with him. We're in no hurry and a great increase in speed brings a huge number of problems."

"What kind of problems?" asked Cynthia.

"Oh—heat, for instance. The outer shell of the rocket would get heated up to such a degree that it might vaporize. Then there are meteorites which are microscopic in size. They won't do any harm at a thousand miles an hour. But they would penetrate a rocket colliding with them at really high speeds and go right through the bodies of the people inside, killing them. They've tried that with monkeys—accelerating particles to huge velocities and directing them at the monkeys. The monkeys died though there wasn't a mark on them. It's curious in a way because our bodies are being penetrated by cosmic radiation and probably cosmic particles as well all the time, but because they travel relatively slowly we suffer no ill effects. Speed them up and they would be fatal. It's actually the principle of the old ray guns we used to read about in comics when we were kids."

"You're sure that you won't be exposed to that kind of danger?"

"No," said Vincent. "Not a chance. We'll just chug along at a nice, steady thousand miles an hour, which is a lot slower than many military planes fly these days, land on the moon, take some photographs, pick up a few rocks and then come on back again. Really, the only reason people think it is so fearful is because it hasn't been done before. Actually our main problem is going to be finding some way to pass the time on the rocket. Kokintz has proposed that we bring along some chessmen and he's going to teach me to play. There'll be certain observations to make of the rocket itself and various celestial bodies. But over and above that, we'll have plenty of leisure."

It was 11 P.M. when Vincent got back to the castle, and its occupants had already retired for the night. He felt much more serene in his mind after his evening with Cynthia. He felt now as if he belonged to someone and was loved by someone, and this gave him a deep strength and self-confidence, very much at odds with his previous state when he had been readily irritated with everybody and most of all with himself.

To enter the castle he had to cross over the drawbridge to go to the courtyard which was contained within the massive outer walls of the castle. The moon was newly risen, throwing an elongated shadow of himself before him across the worn cobblestones of the courtyard.

He looked at it and was amused by the thought that the moon had caused him to grow—at least in his shadow. He turned to look at the moon, sailing silent and impassive in the dark heavens. It was so bright that no stars were to be seen close to it, their light canceled by the moon's glow. The dark markings of the various "seas" of the moon could be plainly seen with mottled light areas around them which Vincent knew to be mountains. Some of them were as high as Mount Everest, or so Dr. Kokintz had told him. It would not be long before he stood on their steep and arid sides, gazing at earth. He shuddered and, turning his back on the moon, strode briskly toward the castle.

The main gate was open and his own quarters lay up a circular stairway to the left. There were four of these circular staircases, one in each corner of the castle, climbing the interior of a tower located at each corner. The staircase in the Jericho Tower, as stated, had been removed so the tower might house the rocket, but the other three staircases were in good repair and constant use.

One only led down to the dungeon—the one up which Vincent was about to climb. As he entered the tower to go up the staircase, switching on a flashlight he had with him, he heard a loud cry from below him in the direction of the dungeon, followed by a great clattering and then another cry. Then there was silence. Vincent darted down the stairs. At the bottom he found Mr. Spender, seated in a terrible litter of broken cameras and holding his head.

"Are you hurt?" cried Vincent, rushing to him and helping him to his feet.

"No," said Mr. Spender. "Not much. Missed my footing, you know, and came clattering down here." He looked around at the wreckage of his cameras and said, "Oh dear. Oh dear. They're all broken. This is terrible."

Vincent felt quite sorry for him. He helped him gather up the pieces and then said, "Whatever were you doing coming down the stairs anyway?"

"I thought I heard an owl," said Mr. Spender.

"In the dungeon?" said Vincent. "Owls go out at night-time. Hunting. What *is* all this about anyway?"

"I'm afraid I've made a mess of things—again," said Mr. Spender. "I throw myself on your mercy and I claim sanctuary." To Vincent's embarrassment, Mr. Spender plumped down and grabbed Vincent around the legs as he said this. But in plumping down, Mr. Spender's knee hit on a sharp piece of one of the broken cameras and he said "Ow," rather spoiling the effect of his appeal.

"What the blazes are you kneeling there for?" asked Vincent. "Get up."

"Not until you promise me sanctuary," said Mr. Spender, rubbing his injured knee with one hand but holding on to Vincent's legs with the other. "You have to do it, you know. It's the law of nations."

"All right," said Vincent, who would have promised anything to get out of his embarrassing predicament. "You can have sanctuary, whatever that is. Now get up and explain all this to me."

Mr. Spender gave a big sigh of relief, got up, dusted off the knees of his hairy tweeds and sat down on the bottom step of the circular staircase, beckoning Vincent to join him.

"I'm not really a bird watcher," he said. "I'm a spy. Of course, I should really be called an intelligence agent, but in the present circumstances . . ." He gestured toward the broken cameras and shrugged his shoulders. "I don't know who is going to pay the bill for them," he said hopelessly. "Not me. I haven't got a cent, really."

"What do you mean you're a spy?" said Vincent, ignoring all the side issues. "Who are you spying for and what do you want to find out?"

"The Russians," said Mr. Spender. "My mother was a Russian, but my father was an Englishman. We lived in Russia for a while and then in Poland and then in India where my father had a government post and used to go exploring and sometimes shoot tigers. It was a wonderful life. I thought I could spend the rest of my life like my father did, if the supply of tigers didn't run out. But when they took India away from us, which meant no more of those wonderful jobs, that put an end to that, and I had to find some other way of making a living.

"I tried all kinds of things. You wouldn't think to look at me that I once owned a little tobacco shop on the beach front in Bournemouth, would you?"

"No," said Vincent, but only because that was the answer patently expected of him.

"Nice little business," said Mr. Spender. "But humdrum. I wanted something exciting and by various means which I won't explain to you now, I became an agent for the Russians. This was my first big assignment."

"What kind of spying did you do before?" asked Vincent.

"Nothing very big," said Mr. Spender. "I really got my start supplying cigarette papers to other agents to write their secret messages on. They're all written on cigarette papers, you know. Then I was asked to go and spy on that American submarine that went to Scotland years ago with the Polaris missile on board."

"What did you have to find out about it?" asked Vincent.

"Oh, I just had to report that it was actually there and so on. Just checking up, you know."

"But, heavens, there were pictures of it in all the newspapers, and students from Scottish universities protesting its presence by swarming all over it."

"Well, the Russians don't believe anything they read in other people's newspapers," said Mr. Spender. "They are a very suspicious people. They hardly believe anything at all. They even check on the work of their own government departments. That's why I was sent here."

"Take your time and explain," said Vincent. "Right now I don't understand a thing."

"Well, they had to check on their own propaganda," said Mr. Spender. "They had to check on whether their propaganda was the truth or not. That would make a big difference."

"Muddier and muddier," said Vincent, "but wade ahead."

"It's very simple," said Mr. Spender. "Their propaganda ministry had put out the story that that fifty million dollars got from the United States was to be spent not on rocket reserach but on plumbing. Now I had to find out whether that was true or whether it wasn't true. And of course I found out that it *was* true—although you did try to stop me."

"Stop you?" cried Vincent. "I thought I was doing everything I could to help you."

"Oh, come now," said Mr. Spender. "I'm being frank with you so you might as well be frank with me. You'll have to admit that you tried to deceive me by pretending that that big thing you have in the tower over there with the pipes sticking out of it was a rocket designed to go to the moon when it is as plain as a pikestaff that it's actually a castle-sized water heater."

"But it isn't a water heater," said Vincent. "It's a rocket designed to go to the moon and it will take off very shortly."

"There you are," said Mr. Spender sorrowfully. "Trying to deceive me again."

"Look," said Vincent, "I'm telling you the truth. If you don't want to accept it, that's up to you. That rocket we are building there is going to go to the moon in about a month. And I'll be aboard it with Dr. Kokintz as I explained to you during your tour this morning."

"It's sad how human beings keep trying to deceive each other," said Mr. Spender. "It makes you feel that life is hardly worth living."

"You're a fine one to talk about deceit," said Vincent. "You come here pretending to be a bird watcher and actually you're a spy."

"Oh, but my profession calls for deceit," said Mr. Spender. "In my business deceit is a virtue whereas with you—well, it's just an unnecessary vice. That is the difference."

"Look," said Vincent, "I don't suppose I can make you believe this, but I'm going to try. We have nothing to hide here. Everything is open. That rocket is actually a rocket being prepared to go to the moon. And the rest of the stuff is just new plumbing fixtures for the castle. The plumbing fixtures are not important. The rocket is. But to show you that I'm not trying to hide anything, you can take all the pictures you want of anything you want. Nobody will try to stop you."

"Can I really?" asked Mr. Spender, brightening immediately. "I say, that's awfully nice of you. Really very generous. I withdraw my request for sanctuary. I don't think, since I have permission to take the pictures, that I have to take refuge from my employers for the time being."

"Think nothing of it," said Vincent. "Now let's go to bed."

The following morning Vincent explained to his father and Dr. Kokintz that Mr. Spender was really a Russian spy come to Grand Fenwick to check the Russian propaganda story that the American grant was for the purpose of modernizing the castle and that the story of building a rocket was actually a pretext designed to put the Soviet Union in an embarrassing international situation.

"I can't get him to believe anything else," Vincent concluded.

"What a pity he really wasn't interested in the bobolinks," said Dr. Kokintz, ignoring the whole issue. "It would be very valuable indeed, in view of the present controversy, to have an independent witness testify to the presence of bobolinks in our forest." He brightened for a moment. "Perhaps Mr. Spender would still consent to come and take a picture of them and testify that they are actually here," he said.

"In view of his attitude toward the rocket," said Vincent, "Mr. Spender is the last person to ask to testify about the bobolinks. He would probably swear they were vultures. He seems incapable of accepting the simple truth."

"It is one of the hazards of espionage," said the Count of Mountjoy. "Spies thrive on what is hidden. If nothing is hidden, they have nothing to thrive on and their situation is desperate."

Mr. Spender spent the whole day taking pictures of the plumbing with a camera Tully lent him. Then he caught the evening bus back to Switzerland, where he spent the next week compiling a report. It was masterly and suited the Soviet propaganda agency to perfection.

His report stated that Grand Fenwick was going to elaborate lengths to disguise the real purpose of the American grant. A rocket, built into one of the towers of Grand Fenwick castle to support the American deceit, was really a water heater and he was pleased to be able to enclose photographs showing the true nature of the work upon which the American money was being spent and for which it had been granted. He enclosed two dozen pictures of the plumbing and the sections of the giant furnace together with several shots of whole rows of bathtubs.

The Soviet Ministry of Propaganda deliberated over the pictures and the report and sent Mr. Spender a draft for two thousand English pounds, and he immediately bought himself a big game gun and a plane fare to India and was not heard of thereafter.

The pictures of the plumbing and the bathtubs, with an article under the heading "American Deceit on Workers Exposed" was printed on the main foreign news page of *Izvestia*.

It was unfortunate that it appeared on the very day that the Grand Fenwick rocket took off for the moon.

XII

The take-off went without a hitch and it is a pity that, due to the world's incredulity, the only witnesses to it were the people of Grand Fenwick. The Count of Mountjoy sent invitations to the launching to the heads of the principal nations of the world but nobody even bothered to reply, which upset him as being impolite.

"Royalty in better times would attend the opening of a bridge," he said. "Presidents these days will not attend the launching of a rocket to the moon. It is all part of the deterioration of our times. A sense of public duty has given way to a sense of political expediency and the whole world suffers from the change."

Headed by Gloriana and her consort Tully Bascomb, the people of the Duchy crowded together in the courtyard around the Jericho Tower, and Dr. Kokintz and Vincent of Mountjoy took their leave of them.

First of all Gloriana made a speech which was short but nonetheless effective. She said that this was a very proud moment in the history of Grand Fenwick, for two men of the nation were going to dare the heavens and be the first of all men on earth to attempt a landing on the moon.

She reminded them that Florence had been only a small state, scarcely the size of Grand Fenwick, when Galileo had, with a telescope he fashioned himself, laid the foundations for the modern science of astronomy. Copernicus was a citizen of one of the poorest countries in Europe when he revolutionized thinking on the subject of the solar system, which men had previously thought rotated about the earth.

"Size of nations has little to do with scientific achievement," she said, "and it has fallen to our lot to lead mankind into outer space. I do not doubt for one moment that this mission will be successful," she continued. "But when our men return to us, let us not be overly proud, but remember that all things are done under the hand of God, and nothing may be achieved by man alone.

"It is proper then that we should ask God's blessing upon this project and recall for our comfort during the period of waiting that lies ahead of us, that all things are in His hands and He is concerned about the falling of a sparrow."

Gloriana glanced at Cynthia Bentner when she said this. Cynthia was standing by Vincent of Mountjoy and her face was very pale. Her lips were trembling and she bent her head and Gloriana looked quickly away from her.

"You can be sure of our prayers," she said, turning to Vincent and Dr. Kokintz. "And the prayers of a whole nation, however small, will hardly go unanswered. We send with you all our faith, all our courage and all our love. With these you will not be alone, even on the distant plateaus of the moon, but supported and surrounded by the spirit of the people of the nation from which you come."

The Bishop of Grand Fenwick then blessed the two astronauts and the rocket, and the people tried to look somewhere else but could not when Vincent took leave of Cynthia. As many as could came forward to shake the astronauts' hands and suddenly they were alone in a little area by themselves, the crowd withdrawing from them.

Dr. Kokintz blinked around in the bright sunlight through his thick glasses and then, turning to Gloriana, said, "Thank you, my lady. We will be back soon, please God."

And then, in silence, they walked to the base of the Jericho Tower and through a heavy steel door which Vincent had had installed there and which was as stout as that on a massive safe. They were about to swing the door closed behind them when Dr. Kokintz opened it again and said to Tully, "Please do not forget to feed the birds." Then the door was shut and those outside heard the several locks on it being slipped into place and knew that in a few minutes Kokintz and Vincent would be entering the rocket and strapping themselves to their bunks in preparation for the take-off.

Everybody now backed away from the tower. They had been told that there was no danger at all, that since the rocket was equipped with nuclear power, there would be no terrible blasts of flame to crack the stones of the tower and burn them, but they could not believe this. Nonetheless they moved to the wall surrounding the courtyard and stared in silence at the Tower of Jericho from which the capstones had all been removed, so that it looked like a huge factory chimney.

There was no warning of the take-off at all—no thunderous noise or escape of vapors in terrifying clouds. Watching the top of the tower, they saw the nose of the rocket appear quite slowly above it, as if it were some creature come out to sniff the morning air. A big "Aaaah" went up from the people; and then in utter silence the rocket suddenly left the tower, so swiftly that they could not follow the motion until it was already many hundreds of feet up in the air.

It left a graceful thin line of vapor behind it, and when it was up some distance, there was a sudden heavy explosion which produced a shock wave that sent the spectators staggering and many of them thought that the rocket had blown up.

"Mach One," said the Count of Mountjoy. "They have gone through the sound barrier."

After a little while the rocket appeared to alter course, as if it were coming down to the earth again. "They're in trouble," someone cried. "It's falling back to earth!"

But it was not so.

The rocket was still gaining altitude and Tully, who was the first to collect his wits, rushed to Dr. Kokintz' study to switch on the microwave two-way radio with which they could communicate with the astronauts. His instructions were not to message them first but to wait for a report, and it was twenty minutes before they got one. Then Dr. Kokintz' voice came through, surprisingly clear, as if he were talking from the next room.

"Everything is fine," he said. "Please announce our successful take-off to the world."

That was the end of the message.

Beyond this one microwave radio set, beamed to the rocket, there were no facilities for fast communication in the Duchy.

Grand Fenwick had no cable office, no telephones and certainly no broadcasting station. A press release had been prepared in advance, however, and it was agreed that this would be sent on the bus to the Associated Press, United Press and Reuters bureaus in Bern as providing the best method of letting the world know that Grand Fenwick was on its way to the moon.

The Swiss bus driver was a little more regular in his schedule than the French bus driver who served the northern border of the Duchy, which was the reason Bern was selected. But he had had a flat tire that morning and his bus was an hour behind schedule when he stopped at the border of the Duchy. He was met there by the Count of Mountjoy, who was dancing with irritation at the delay.

"You *would* have to have a flat tire on the day we sent a rocket to the moon," said the Count unreasonably.

"If I'd known about it, I would have put new tires on all the wheels," said the bus driver. He glanced past the Count of Mountjoy down the road leading into Grand Fenwick, which he had never visited and had no desire to visit. "Is everybody crazy in there?" he asked. "Or is it only you?"

Then he slammed the door shut and revved up the engine before Mountjoy could think of an appropriate reply.

Bern was only fifty miles by road from the Grand Fenwick frontier, but because of the flat tire and rather heavy traffic at Neuchâtel (it was market day) it was four hours before the news of the Grand Fenwick expedition to the moon reached the news agencies in that city. And then there was more delay.

It is unfortunately true of news agencies that they regard anything that comes by bus and is contained in an envelope as not being news. So at the Associated Press, United Press and Reuters bureaus, where the three releases were delivered by messenger from the bus station, the envelopes were put aside to be opened by the office boy whose chore it was to pull out anything from the mail that might be worked up into a feature story or used as a "mailer"—that is, a little feature story itself distributed by mail to their various clients rather than over the teletype.

Reuters was, of course, the senior news agency and it is well known among newspapermen that Reuters has a genius for getting scoops in the unlikeliest places. It is also well known among newspapermen that Reuters, when it gets moving on a story, moves faster than any other agency. Part of this is undoubtedly due to a special *esprit de corps* among Reuters men, who think of themselves as envoys of Britain and do not like to let their country down. In short, the reporter who fails Reuters fails not merely a news agency but a nation, and this spirit had trickled down to the office boy of the Reuters agency at Bern, who had secret dreams of opening the mail and uncovering some sensational scoop, like a plot to assassinate the President of the United States or put strychnine in the feed of a Derby favorite.

The Reuters office boy was the first to open the dispatch from Grand Fenwick. He did it immediately after lunch and before hunting up the tea things to prepare the cup of tea that the Reuters staff would have out of thick white cups at three o'clock that afternoon.

He picked the Grand Fenwick dispatch out of the bundle of mail because the envelope was king-size and had a fascinating crest on it and he thought it might be an invitation to attend some embassy ball and his boss would be busy and would tell him to go instead. . . . The office boy's daydreams were not confined to an assassination plot directed against the President of the United States or a scheme to doctor the feed of a Derby favorite. The Reuters office boy opened the big envelope from Grand Fenwick and his eyes bugged at what he read. For what he read exceeded all the great scoops of all his daydreams, which he would one time pluck from the routine mail, making his name famous among the great newspapermen of the world.

The heading on the first sheet of paper in the envelope (there were two of them) read:

MOON ROCKET LAUNCHED

And below was the following statement:

The Duchy of Grand Fenwick announced today the successful launching of a rocket designed to land two men on the moon, the launching taking place from the Tower of Jericho in the Castle of Grand Fenwick.

Two astronauts were aboard the rocket—Dr. Theodore Kokintz, world-renowned physicist, and Vincent of Mountjoy, son of the Count of Mountjoy, Prime Minister of the Duchy. The launching occurred at 9:15 A.M. [the date had been filled in since the release was prepared ahead of time] and went off without a hitch. The rocket, powered by an element discovered in the Duchy's famous Pinot Grand Fenwick wine, is expected to arrive on the moon nine days and four hours from the time of launching.

The rocket has been designed to travel at a comparatively low speed—no more than a thousand miles an hour—thus avoiding the many problems attached to high-speed travel in space. . . .

When he had read this far, the office boy, trembling, took the release over to the chief correspondent's desk.

"Sir," he said in great excitement, "I think this is important."

"What is it?" asked the correspondent, busy at his typewriter and not even bothering to look up.

"Grand Fenwick has launched a rocket to the moon," said the office boy.

"From the Tower of Jericho," said the correspondent. "For the love of Mike, when are you going to catch on?"

"It *is* from the Tower of Jericho," said the office boy, blushing. "And the launching was at nine-fifteen this morning. Dr. Kokintz was aboard . . ."

At the mention of the name of Dr. Kokintz, the correspondent looked up at the office boy and said, "Give me that," and snatched the papers out of the boy's hand. He read it, threw it down on his desk and stroked his chin.

"Wonder who on AP dreamed this one up," he said. "Let me see the envelope this thing came in." The boy produced the envelope and the correspondent inspected it carefully, noting the Grand Fenwick crest.

"It's their envelope all right," he said. "But anyone can get hold of one of them."

"It's signed by the Count of Mountjoy," said the office boy.

"I'm not blind," said the correspondent rudely. But nonetheless he inspected the signature.

"I think it's legitimate," said the boy, greatly daring.

"Horse feathers," said the correspondent. "It's just Joe Redditch over at AP. Forget about it."

The office boy went away, crushed. Here was the great scoop which he had dreamed would one day come through the mail, and it was a joke. He looked at the crest on the envelope again and then at the signature of the Count of Mountjoy. Then he ducked out of the office, got on his bicycle and pelted through the traffic to the bus station. There he pestered several people until he found the driver of the bus which had passed Grand Fenwick that morning.

"Did you pick up anything from Grand Fenwick to bring to Bern this morning?" he asked.

"Yes," said the bus driver. "Three letters. Given me by a real nut. He said they'd sent a rocket to the moon."

"Thanks," said the boy, and then as an afterthought asked, "What did he look like?"

"Tall. Silver-haired. Had a monocle," said the bus driver.

"Who were the letters for?" the boy persisted.

"Reuters, Associated Press and United Press," said the bus driver.

"There was one for Associated Press too?" asked the boy.

"Yes," said the bus driver.

The boy didn't wait for more. He jumped on his bicycle and rode full speed back to the office, where he presented himself, out of breath, at the chief correspondent's desk again.

"I checked on that moon rocket, sir," he said. "And it's true. I went to the bus station. The driver said the letter came from Grand Fenwick. It was given to him personally by a man who was tall and silver-haired and wore a monocle. There was one for United Press and one for Associated Press as well."

The mention of his rivals stimulated the correspondent to action. He picked up the dispatch again, glanced at the clock and went dubiously to the teletype by which he could transmit messages direct to London. He sat down in the little swivel chair before it and stared at the keys. Then he put Mountjoy's dispatch in the copy holder, hesitated and hit the signal key to call London's attention to the fact that he had something to transmit. The teletype printed out the letters

G.A. for "Go Ahead" from London. Shrugging his shoulders, the correspondent started his message.

HAVE TIP HERE THAT NUCLEAR-POWERED ROCKET LAUNCHED TO MOON FROM GRAND FENWICK STOP [he typed] NO COMMUNICATIONS POSSIBLE WITH DUCHY STOP. KNOW THIS SOUNDS CRAZY BUT CAN JODRELL BANK CONFIRM IF ROCKET HAS TAKEN OFF STOP. SPEED ONE THOUSAND MILES PER HOUR, TAKE-OFF AT 9:15 A.M. STOP. WAGNER.

They waited for a few minutes and then the teletype started to clatter, the keys rapping out the message from London.

TOWER OF JERICHO I SUPPOSE STOP. WILL CHECK ANYWAY AND MESSAGE YOU STOP. REDGROVE.

"Well," said the correspondent, "they'll be telling that story about my message in all the pubs in Fleet Street in half an hour. Shouldn't wonder if I got fired." He glared at the office boy, who felt uncomfortable and guilty and glanced at the clock and went off to make the tea, as being the best thing to do in the circumstances.

Ten minutes later the teletype started to chatter again, this time giving first of all the six sharp rings that signified an urgent message was coming through. Everyone in the office hearing the rings gathered around the machine watching anxiously as the keys clattered out the words.

JODRELL GREENWICH AND OTHERS REPORT ROCKET TAKE-OFF FROM SOMEWHERE SOUTHERN FRANCE STOP. FILE ALL YOU HAVE ON GRAND FENWICK STOP. WE WILL HOLD HERE PENDING CONFIRMATION. URGENT. REDGROVE.

"Here," shouted the chief correspondent to one of the assistants, handing him the Grand Fenwick statement, "put that on the wire—all of it. Mark it *hold* until I send confirmation. I'm off to Grand Fenwick." He fled from the office, dived into his car and headed for the Duchy.

One of the duties of the office boy at the Associated Press bureau in Bern, which was in the same building, was to keep an eye on the Reuters office boy and, if he saw him going out of the building urgently, to find out what was his errand. On this occasion the AP boy goofed, for he was playing a game of checkers with one of the junior reporters.

The Reuters man reached Grand Fenwick in one hour of perilous driving, got a quick interview with the Count of

Mountjoy and Tully Bascomb, found nobody had bothered to photograph the take-off of the rocket, but got a picture of its construction taken by Tully, denounced the Duchy for not having a single phone in its territory, and stormed back into Switzerland, where he called his London office from Neuchâtel.

"Redgrove," he said when he got hold of the chief of the London Bureau, "release that Grand Fenwick rocket story. It's astounding, impossible, crazy . . . anything you want to say about it .But it's true. I've got a picture of the rocket I'm going to put on the wire when I finish phoning you. We've got a clear beat on this. AP and UP haven't woken up yet."

"Get back to Grand Fenwick and stay there and keep a story running," said Redgrove. "What are communications like?"

"There are none," said Redgrove. "No phones or cable offices. I'm calling from Neuchâtel in Switzerland. I'll call Bern and have them send me a couple of men to establish a messenger relay system. If you want to message me, do it through the post office in Neuchâtel."

"Can you give any more details now beyond those you sent over the wire?" asked Redgrove.

"Yes," said the chief correspondent. "Give me a telephonist."

Reuters, in common with the whole British press, employed highly skilled shorthand writers who could take any dictated story over a long-distance telephone as fast as it was rattled out to them. A telephonist was put on the wire and the Reuters correspondent, long-practiced at this work, dictated an impromptu story of the short radio report from the rocket to Grand Fenwick, details of Gloriana's farewell address, reaction in the Duchy to the rocket's take-off and the picturesque detail that Dr. Kokintz' last words before departing for the moon, had been a request that his birds be taken care of and fed regularly.

Within a matter of a few minutes, teletypes in newspaper, radio and television offices all over the world, from Darjeeling to Detroit and Melbourne to Manchester, were giving the six abrupt, spine-tingling rings that indicated that a dispatch of the first urgency was coming over the line. And then all these teletypes in all these offices all over the world began batting out the words:

URGENT—A NUCLEAR-POWERED ROCKET WITH TWO MEN ABOARD, ONE OF THEM WORLD-FAMOUS PHYSICIST DR. THEODORE KOKINTZ, WAS SUCCESSFULLY LAUNCHED FROM THE

DUCHY OF GRAND FENWICK AT 9:15 GMT THIS MORNING IN
AN ATTEMPT TO LAND ON THE MOON. . . .

The story, delivered in short takes of one paragraph for
quick handling, ran to several columns of copy.

It was ripped off the teletypes as it came through, paragraph by paragraph.

Radio and television programs were interrupted to put it
immediately on the air. Newspapers replated, flinging extra
editions out on the streets in every city of the globe, and
suddenly it was as if the whole distracted world had been
silenced and all eyes and ears were directed toward the tiny
little Duchy tucked away in the Northern Alps between
France and Switzerland which had performed this miracu-
lous and unbelievable feat.

The news hit the eastern border of the United States about
eight in the evening, when the last editions of the New York
evening papers had long been put to bed. Nonetheless they
called their staffs back, replated and put out extras.

The White House Press Secretary, who was having a drink
at the Press Club bar in Washington, got the story hot off
the Reuters teletype, which was conveniently installed only
a few steps from the bar. When the six warning bells rang,
the bar emptied and everybody crowded around the Reuters
machine. Somebody read the message aloud as it was pecked
out by the keys and suddenly there was a mass exodus as cor-
respondents and local men dashed back to their offices in
case they should be needed for a Washington reaction.

The White House Press Secretary's name was O'Hara.
He'd left Boston newspapers for Boston politics and, having
astutely handled press relations for the right candidate,
wound up in the White House. In his college days he had
been a champion sprinter, but he broke all his previous rec-
ords in a dash from the Press Club Building to the White
House, flung himself behind his desk and called the President, who was sitting down to dinner with an ambassador
from one of the Arab States.

"Chief," he said, "there's a Reuters report just come in that
the Duchy of Grand Fenwick has successfully launched a
rocket to the moon with Kokintz aboard. The press are
going to be down on us like an avalanche in a minute."

"Say that again," said the President.

O'Hara repeated the statement again and asked if there
was any comment he could give from the White House.

"Comment?" cried the astounded President. "Comment?
Just what would you suggest, O'Hara? I say it's crazy."

"That's what I thought, Chief," said O'Hara. "But there

are too many details for it to be anything but true. We ought to have some comment ready. I think we ought to say that we welcome this splendid achievement and so on and point out that, without wishing to detract in any way from Grand Fenwick's credit, we loaned them the money for the research and gave them a Saturn rocket as a space vehicle."

There was a terrible silence while the President digested the import of this last statement.

"Are you losing your mind, O'Hara?" he said at last. "Don't you know what this means? It means that using a secondhand rocket which we gave them, and with an expenditure of a miserable fifty-million dollars, Grand Fenwick has beaten us to the moon. That's what it means."

"They're not there yet, Chief," said O'Hara. "They're not much more than ten thousand miles on their way. It's a slow rocket," he added.

"Ten thousand miles is a heck of a lot farther than we have been able to send a monkey," said the President. He pulled himself together. "No comment," he said. "Tell them we're awaiting confirmation through official sources. And I want a full-dress cabinet meeting here in an hour. That's not for release," he added.

O'Hara just had time to call the President's chief assistant about the cabinet meeting before the telephone calls from press, radio and television started to pour in. To all he gave the stock reply that the President was awaiting official confirmation of the report and until this was received there would be no comment from the White House. But he was not let off easily.

The newspapermen had been digging into the clippings about Grand Fenwick and found the previous stories announcing the gift of $50,000,000 to Grand Fenwick for rocket research and later the transfer of a Saturn rocket to the Duchy.

What about it? they wanted to know. How come Grand Fenwick could send a rocket to the moon with a gift of what amounted to petty cash and the cast-off materials of the United States? O'Hara pointed out that those questions should be properly addressed either to the State Department or to the National Aeronautics and Space Administration. The tone of the press was indignant and, sensing this, O'Hara called the editors of such papers as the *New York Times*, the *Kansas City Star* and the *Christian Science Monitor* and suggested that they might consider withholding editorial comment involving the United States for a day or two. The editors agreed. But when a special edition of the *New York*

Daily News, which had been flown to Washington, was brought to O'Hara, the headline made him flinch.

It read:

LILLIPUT HEADS FOR MOON
IN JUNKED U.S. ROCKET

The *New York Daily Mirror* headline was no more friendly. It read:

U.S. "DUD" BECOMES
SPACESHIP FOR DUCHY

"There is going to be hell to pay for this," said O'Hara, eying these headlines. And then he began wondering grimly what it would be like back at his old post writing editorials for the paper in Boston. He shuddered at the prospect.

XIII

By the time the astonished members of the President's cabinet had assembled in the White House, official confirmation of the launching of the Grand Fenwick rocket had come through. It came from the U. S. Ambassador to Switzerland, through the legation in Bern, which had sent a messenger scurrying to Grand Fenwick to check on the report as soon as it came over the Swiss radio.

The President confronted his cabinet grimly with this official confirmation received by telephone by the Secretary of State.

"There is no sense in trying to tone down or underplay in any way the massive defeat we have suffered at the hands of Grand Fenwick by their incredible success," he said. "We have been concentrating all our resources on making a lunar landing for the past ten years. We have had every facility available to us and unlimited funds. We have been beaten by a nation of five thousand people using a secondhand rocket and with a budget of only fifty million dollars—which they got from us. You've seen the headlines in the New York tabloids, I suppose."

They nodded glumly.

"Well, that's the kind of reaction we can expect from the whole nation," said the President. "And I might add, the whole world. We have suffered a tremendous blow to our prestige and, whether we deserve it or not, will have to endure it. What I want to know is why nobody informed me of what was happening in Grand Fenwick.

"Why do I always have to be taken by surprise like this? Why does the administration and the whole nation have to suffer this sudden and overwhelming assault on its prestige? Wasn't there anyone in this room—anyone among you gentlemen who are concerned with every phase of our foreign affairs, our military defense and our space program—anyone at all who had an inkling of what was going on in Grand Fenwick?"

The cabinet members looked uneasily at each other but made no reply.

"I don't understand it," said the President. "I may live the rest of my life and never understand it. How can this little nation keep such a momentous project secret right up to the last second so as to astound the world, and we, a very big nation indeed, seem to be incapable of keeping anything secret at all? That's what I'd like to know."

The Secretary of State cleared his throat. The major fault, he felt, rested with him, and his New England upbringing demanded that he accept the blame.

"They didn't try to keep it a secret, Mr. President," he said. "They plainly, publicly and many times announced that they were going to try to send a rocket to the moon. Nobody believed them. The fault, if it is anybody's, is primarily mine. In his initial letter asking for a loan, the Count of Mountjoy stated plainly that the object of the loan was to enter the space race by devising a rocket to send to the moon. And to buy a fur coat for the Duchess Gloriana XII."

"A fur coat for the Duchess?" echoed the President, who had not been aware of this paragraph in Mountjoy's letter.

"Yes," said the Secretary of State. "Five million dollars for a rocket and fifty thousand dollars for a fur coat. How was I to take that seriously?

"I consulted with my advisers and we came to the conclusion that the request was only a blind—that the real objective was to install bathtubs in the Castle of Grand Fenwick, while at the same time providing us with an excuse for lending the money by bringing a third and neutral power into the space race. Five million was ridiculous for rocket research. So I upped it to fifty million."

The President covered his face with his hands and groaned. "You made them take forty-five million more?" he asked.

"Yes," said the Secretary of State, "I did. We never lend a sum as small as five million," he added. "It is too paltry."

"I don't understand about this fur coat," said the President after a little silence.

"I don't understand about it either," said the Secretary of State. "I find that I am incapable of divining the intentions of the Duchy of Grand Fenwick, and I feel that I should tender my resignation, effective at whatever time is convenient to yourself."

The President shook his head wearily. "I don't think that is necessary," he said. "I'm not looking for scapegoats and I don't think that you are any more to blame than any of the rest of us here. What I still don't understand is how at no time at all did any of us—even our highly specialized technical staffs—suspect that Grand Fenwick was seriously engaged in rocket research."

"There was an invitation to the rocket launching addressed to yourself through me," said the Secretary of Defense. "I assumed that it would be a propaganda launching—that at the last moment it would be canceled or a misfire would be staged, and so did not bother to reply."

"Why did you assume that?" asked the President.

"What else was there to assume, Chief?" asked the Secretary of Defense. "How were we to suspect that they were actually going to launch a rocket to the moon? What clues did we have that we could take seriously?

"There was a grant of fifty million dollars. That's not enough to get a manned rocket to the moon and back again, starting from scratch. There was Kokintz. Well, to be sure he is the outstanding man in his field. But could we assume that one lone man was a match for the corps of top physicists, chemists, mathematicians and engineers we have at our disposal who have been working on the project for more than a decade? Certainly not. There weren't any grounds to suspect for one moment that they were actually engaged in rocket research. Why, they didn't even go through the basic step of orbiting a sputnik first."

"Not even as much as a wine bottle," said the Secretary of State.

"A wine bottle?" cried Dr. Fritz Meidel, who had also been summoned to the meeting. "A wine bottle! Oh my God!"

"What about a wine bottle?" demanded the President, turning on him.

"When we were checking Hotfoot off Ascension Island a couple of months ago," said Dr. Meidel, "a wine bottle fell out of the sky into the ocean and we picked it up. We figured that it had been dropped by one of the planes providing an umbrella overhead."

"Well, hadn't it?" asked the President.

"I don't think so—now," said Dr. Meidel. "I remember the label on the wine bottle. It was Pinot Grand Fenwick. I thought at the time it was odd that one of our plane pilots should be carrying a bottle of so rare a wine in his plane. But I had too many things to attend to and it all slipped my mind."

"Now that it has all come back to your mind," said the President testily, "what about the wine bottle?"

"It wasn't just a wine bottle, Mr. President," said Dr. Meidel. "It was a sputnik—put into orbit by Grand Fenwick. It can have been nothing else."

"You mean they orbited a wine bottle?" demanded the President, aghast.

"Yes," said Dr. Meidel. "It's as good an object for orbiting as a solid gold sphere—and costs less."

"What happened to it?" asked the President after a moment of shocked silence.

"Senator Ridgeway took it home and gave it to one of his kids as a souvenir."

The President groaned. "That about puts it in a nutshell," he said. "Grand Fenwick orbits a wine bottle. It is picked up as a souvenir for a school kid. Grand Fenwick announces its plans to send a rocket to the moon. Everybody believes they're actually installing bathtubs. Grand Fenwick invites us to the launching of the rocket. We don't even bother to reply. Then Grand Fenwick launches the rocket—and here we all are, caught flatfooted. Completely unprepared."

"The Russians are in the same boat," said the Secretary of State tentatively. "It's a terrible blow to us. But it's a terrible blow to them too. I don't think that anyone can fairly accuse me of being unpatriotic. But in a way I'm glad Grand Fenwick succeeded. If we'd made it first, or the Russians had made it first . . ." He shrugged and did not finish the sentence, knowing that the purport of what he had in mind was clear enough.

"The trouble with the Russians," said the Secretary of Defense, "is that they will probably never announce to their people that Grand Fenwick reached the moon."

"That's true," said Dr. Meidel. "There has been very little mention in the Russian press even of the various big successes we have achieved so far. They may decide to utterly suppress the Grand Fenwick feat as being too much of a blow to their prestige for them to absorb."

"We're getting a little ahead of ourselves," said the Defense Secretary. "The Grand Fenwick rocket hasn't got to the moon *yet*. It won't get there for about nine days. Anything can happen to it in the meantime."

The President turned to Dr. Meidel. "What do you think?" he asked. "What are its chances?"

"I can't say," said Dr. Meidel. "I haven't enough to go on. I have only what I heard over the radio and read in these papers here. But the basic problem of space exploration has always been fuel. Our fuels are all of the combustion type —dependent upon burning oxygen with various other chemicals to provide thrust. The oxygen has to be taken with the rocket because there isn't any in outer space.

"If Grand Fenwick has indeed devised a nuclear fuel, they are twenty years ahead of our research and Russia's too. I'd say that if they have a nuclear fuel they can get to the moon and back again as readily as I can board a train, go to New York and return."

"From what you've heard and read about this in the last couple of hours, is this fuel feasible?" asked the President.

"Certainly," said Dr. Meidel.

"Do you believe that Grand Fenwick has such a fuel?"

"Made from a hogshead of wine and a barrel full of iron filings," grumbled the Defense Secretary, who was in a bad temper.

"Mr. President," said Dr. Meidel, ignoring the Defense Secretary, "will you use that telephone there to find out whether the Grand Fenwick rocket is still on its way?" The President looked at him dubiously, pressed a button on the telephone and was connected with O'Hara.

"Is the Grand Fenwick rocket still climbing?" he asked, listened for a few seconds, grunted, and put the telephone down.

"It's still on its way," he said. "The last report is from Woomera in Australia and says the rocket is maintaining a steady speed away from the earth. The speed is still one thousand miles an hour."

"Then I'd say that Grand Fenwick has a nuclear fuel as is claimed," said Dr. Meidel. "The speed is the real clue. We have to blast off at tremendous speeds to get up sufficient acceleration to carry us beyond earth's gravity. Our rockets actually fire charges which project them forward like artillery shells. A speed of a thousand miles an hour with an oxygen-based fuel would be ridiculous. The oxygen would all be gone before the rocket got out of the gravitational pull of the earth.

"Plainly the Grand Fenwick rocket has plenty of power available and is just keeping up sufficient thrust to overcome gravity and yet remain below a speed that would provide friction problems for the Saturn. It's quite probable that they'll make it to the moon. About getting back I don't know. There are a thousand hazards involved which they seem to be blithely ignoring."

"What kind of hazards?" asked the President.

"Well," said Dr. Meidel, "there's the nature of the moon's surface to start with. What is it like? Is it buried under a mile of fine dust as some think?

"Even if it is solid, how solid is it? It is composed, at least in part, of hard, igneous rocks or of some crumbling material which might cause the rocket to tip over on its side on landing so that it could not be launched again?

"Then there's the matter of temperature. On the side of the moon exposed to the sun, the temperatures are like those of an electric furnace. On the night side, they are far below anything experienced on earth—even in our polar regions. If the rocket is exposed to the furnace heat of the lunar day followed—without any cooling period—by the absolute cold of lunar night, there is a possibility of the metal collapsing or cracking into a thousand pieces.

"These are some of the hazards. And these, as you know, Mr. President, are some of the reasons why our own lunar project has gone forward slowly and cautiously. Our plan has been, and remains, to orbit several space stations around the moon, first with instruments and then with men, to report on landing conditions. We will land ahead of our own astronauts all the instruments and apparatus needed for their safety when they themselves land on the moon.

"Whatever Grand Fenwick has done, I do not see that we could have proceeded in any other way, or should proceed in any other way. The Russians' program, as far as we know (and we know a great deal about it), follows pretty closely to our own approach." He smiled wryly. "Science does not bow to economic philosophies," he said. "Capitalist and Communist have to solve the same scientific problem in the same manner."

The President felt a prickle of irritation at the last remark, which struck him as being smug. "Grand Fenwick seems to have discovered differently," he snapped. "They just went ahead with a simple plan—to land on the moon —with our money and our rocket." The Defense Secretary was about to remark that it was their wine, but sensing the atmosphere was wrong, held his peace.

The President glared around at the members of the cabinet, for he well knew what the public reaction was going to be. The public wasn't now going to be satisfied with the cautious step-by-step approach, involving the expenditure of billions, which the United States had followed to date. Nor was the public going to be mollified by the fact that the

Soviet Union hadn't gotten to the moon either. The great question to which an answer was going to be demanded was going to be: How can Grand Fenwick get to the moon with fifty million dollars when the United States can't get there with a hundred times that expenditure? And the question immediately following that would be: When will the United States send a manned rocket to the moon?

The President put that question squarely to Dr. Meidel. "Just when can we expect to land on the moon?" he asked.

"In a year's time, Mr. President," replied the scientist smoothly.

"What about next week?" demanded the President.

"Next week?"

"Yes. Haven't we got anything ready to send to the moon now—faster than the Grand Fenwick rocket, so that we can get there first? Just what have we got? A whole lot of plans and instruments and data and no rocket that will do the job?"

"We have the rocket, Mr. President," said Dr. Meidel. "We've had it for two years. But it would be unscientific to dump all our careful preparations and just take off for the moon merely to get there ahead of the Duchy of Grand Fenwick. Unscientific and extremely wasteful."

"Unscientific and extremely effective," the President snapped. "I don't want to underestimate the value of your work and of the various scientists associated with you. I know that it's all very important—to scientists. I don't pretend for one moment that it isn't important to humanity either. But I am not the President of a nation of scientists but of people who have been paying out high taxes for a long time for space research and who will want to know (and rightly) how come we were beaten. They'll want to know how Grand Fenwick got there with last year's wine crop, and we couldn't get there with the whole United States economy.

"The prestige value of making the first lunar landing is enormous. It is quite beyond anybody's ability to calculate. The American people have the right to that prestige and sorely need it in the world today. And so I ask you —why can't we send a manned rocket to the moon right now and get there ahead of Grand Fenwick? I'd like to hear what you gentlemen have to say on that subject."

"You already have my views," said Dr. Meidel. "I think it would be the foolish throwing away of enormous research benefits in favor of—of a childish gesture."

The President grunted and looked at the Secretary of State. "What do you think?" he asked.

"I think it is already too late, Mr. President," he said. "A country as big as ours entering into a sort of spatial footrace with a little nation like Grand Fenwick is undignified, to say the least. If we got to the moon first, we would be the big bully that pushed the little boy aside and snatched the prize. World reaction would be unfavorable to us and I think justly so.

"Furthermore, Mr. President, let us not lose sight of what has been always a larger objective with us—our constantly reiterated and sincere desire to internationalize the conquest of space. If we compete with Grand Fenwick now, we give the lie to all that has been said with sincerity, before the United Nations and the world."

The others nodded their agreement.

"We get a black eye, but we have to take it," said the Secretary of State. "We can legitimately point out that the Grand Fenwick triumph was made possible by United States funds. It looks very bad for us now, I know. There's going to be a lot of angry public reaction. But later our aid will loom larger without any special propaganda effort on our part. Nations will begin to appreciate that our funds don't always have a tag attached to them; and in the long run it is possible that we may benefit, internationally, from Grand Fenwick having gotten to the moon first more than if we had got there first ourselves. As you know, Mr. President, in international affairs, it's the long run that matters. Short-term gains are soon forgotten and not worth the effort."

The President grunted a dubious approval of these arguments and turned to the Defense Secretary. "What do you think?" he asked.

"I have to look at this from the point of view of the Russian reaction," said the Defense Secretary. "Getting to the moon isn't just a scientific and propaganda achievement. It's a military achievement. The moon represents a huge space platform that can be used for military purposes. I think we've fooled around with the scientific aspects far too long and in far too great a detail and forgotten the military aspects. You can bet the Russians will attempt a lunar landing as soon as they can now. And I think we should do the same.

"Dr. Meidel tells us that they've been taking the slow, deliberate scientific approach as we have been doing. This alters the whole thing. They'll want to get there as fast as they can, to establish a national claim to the moon. They won't give a hoot for the Grand Fenwick claim. They're likely to argue that Grand Fenwick's success will inevitably lead to our making an all-out assault. I say that we should get a manned rocket to the moon and we should get it there as fast as we can. Tomorrow, if that is possible."

"I have to warn you that there would be grave risks involved for the astronauts concerned—risks I would not like to be called upon to ask them to take," said Dr. Meidel.

"Aw nuts," said the Secretary of Defense, who for many years had chafed under the cautious approach of the scientific hierarchy of government. "What kind of a state is this country in if we can't ask some of our young men to take a calculated risk on behalf of the United States? I know that any of the men we have trained as astronauts would leap at the chance. They are sick of delays and being fitted into space suits and asked whether they chafe them under the arms or are too tight across the seat. They'd go this very minute if we asked them and thank us for the honor."

"Well," said the President, "when could we be ready for the take-off?"

"Blast-off," said Dr. Meidel, who liked the sporty vernacular of the rocket man. "I'll have to check, Mr. President. I can't answer that question off the cuff. It is all very well for some to talk about scientific fussiness, but a rocket such as our Saturn Mark Two is a more complicated piece of apparatus than a city like New York with all its telephone, electrical and other services. Then there's the weather factor . . ."

"Bah," snorted the Defense Secretary. "Columbus didn't wait on the weather."

"I was wondering when somebody was going to mention Columbus," said the Secretary of State.

"What's your best guess, Doctor?" asked the President, pressing mercilessly for a commitment.

"A week—maybe ten days," replied Meidel.

"I feel that I should warn you again, sir, about making a spectacle of ourselves by entering before the world into a space race with Grand Fenwick," said the Secretary of State. "We will be accused of exactly what we are trying to avoid being accused of—determination to dominate outer space in our own national interests."

"I think we should keep one thing clearly before us, gentlemen," said the President. "Since we have so far found it impossible to achieve a reliable agreement with the Soviet Union over the internationalizing of space, domination is the only path left open to us. Either we dominate or they do and if that's what the choice is, it is going to be us."

The Defense Secretary shifted in his seat, took out a

cigarette, examined it thoughtfully and tamped the tobacco in it by tapping the end against the polished top of the conference table. He was a big, heavy-set man with a forth-right way of talking which people often took for rudeness or bad temper. But behind the bluntness of his speech there was often considerable subtlety of mind and he displayed some of that subtlety now.

"We could say that our object is to help Grand Fenwick," he said, examining the end of the tamped cigarette carefully.

"Help Grand Fenwick?" echoed the President.

"Sure," said the Defense Secretary. "We're not trying to get there first or compete with them in any way. But going to the moon is a dangerous business. We are just going to send a rocket there to stand by and see that the Grand Fenwick boys don't get into any trouble. It's just a matter of being available in case they need us.

"Of course, there isn't anything to stop us raising Old Glory on the moon if we happen to get there first. And the chances are that we will get there first—about two and a half hours after blast-off. But that's not our object. Our object is to render assistance to our Grand Fenwick friends in case they need it." He took a long pull on his cigarette, stubbed it out in the ash tray and looked mildly around him, as if to see whether everybody had understood what he had in mind.

"By thunder! That sounds like the best idea that's come up yet," said the President. "We ought to be clear about one thing, though. Do we get to the moon before Grand Fenwick or after them?"

"Before," said the Secretary of Defense with a slight smile. "We announce, however, that our effort is to render assistance, if needed, to the Grand Fenwick astronauts. We emphasize that we are not trying to beat Grand Fenwick to the moon. But factors of weather, rocket speed, and so on may result in our arriving on the moon first—though our object is international co-operation and help for another country."

"I'm for that," said the Secretary of State. "It would be a tremendous gesture and enormously add to our prestige and demonstrate that we actually are capable of getting to the moon."

"Do we make a public announcement?" asked the President.

"Sure, Chief," said the Defense Secretary. "Have a press conference tomorrow, extend our hearty congratulations to Grand Fenwick, mention that it was American money and aid that made the feat possible, stress that we were seeking internationalization of space and so on. And then say smoothly that we will be sending a rocket of our own to the moon to stand by in case the Grand Fenwick rocket gets into trouble."

"It will immediately allay all the public anger about being beaten by Grand Fenwick," said the Secretary of State.

"Okay," said the President. He turned to Dr. Meidel. "Get the rocket and the men ready," he said. "You've got the ball now. Don't fumble it."

The news of the take-off of the Grand Fenwick rocket reached Russia through the Tass radio monitoring service as well as the Reuters teletype in the offices of *Pravda.*

It produced no national sensation as in the United States for the reason that the people were kept ignorant of the event and in any case had been informed only that morning by *Pravda* that the Grand Fenwick effort was a massive propaganda bid by the American imperialists, the money having actually been spent on bathtubs.

That the money had not been spent on bathtubs provided as much of a shock to the Government of the Soviet Union as it did to the Government of the United States.

A crisis meeting of the Soviet cabinet was immediately held, paralleling that held in the White House. The discussion followed much the same lines as the American conference. The Defense Secretary pressed for the sending of a Russian rocket immediately to the moon to get ahead of the Grand Fenwick rocket. The Commissar for Foreign Affairs argued that this might be resented in Albania—a nation the Soviet Union was having some trouble keeping in line.

It was the Minister for Propaganda who supplied the solution. "Let us send a rocket there to help our comrade workers in the Duchy of Grand Fenwick," he said. "No exception can be taken to that."

"Does our rocket arrive there before the Grand Fenwick rocket?" asked one of the members of the cabinet.

"Before," said the Minister of Defense, "but we point out that we are only trying to be helpful—to assist our comrade astronauts from Grand Fenwick."

"Comrade workers," someone interrupted. "We must beware of cultism."

"There is nothing to stop us raising the Glorious Flag of the Revolution on the moon after we arrive first—which we shall do," said the Minister of Defense.

"What do we do about the *Pravda* story on the bath-tubs?" somebody asked.

"We will attribute it to American sources and expose it as a capitalist lie," was the reply.

And so Russia and the United States readied high-velocity rockets to get to the moon ahead of Grand Fenwick. Meanwhile the Grand Fenwick rocket plugged steadily on into space at a thousand miles an hour.

XIV

Vincent of Mountjoy found the journey to the moon somewhat tedious although it was exciting enough in the first couple of days. He had been fascinated to watch through the retro-periscopes with which the rocket was equipped, the earth revolving magnificently below them, its continents gleaming with platinum brightness in the sun when not obscured by cloud. But after a while the sight paled and he began to feel like a man who was condemned to sit in a planetarium for a long period watching the astronomical display upon its dome.

He had never taken much interest in astronomy and though he was surprised at the blackness of the heavens once they were fairly on their way, and the intensity with which the stars burned in that blackness, and was enchanted by the softer glow of the planets, weaving their way across the void, he finally became bored by it all. Nor was there much about the mechanism of the rocket to keep him busy. The mechanism was basically simple and it all worked. There was nothing for him to do but the cooking and cleaning up, disposing of the tin cans out of which their meals came through pressurized ports of a design somewhat similar to torpedo tubes.

Unfortunately the microwave radio with which they had intended to communicate daily with Grand Fenwick failed after the first few hours of flight. It would neither receive nor send and Dr. Kokintz, after examining it, announced that it had become radioactive as a result of the Pinotium 64 fuel which, with the bin of iron filings, powered the rocket.

"It will probably work again when we reach the moon and the reactor is turned off. Until then . . ." He shrugged and looked a little sad. "I had not thought to be so long without news of the bobolinks," he said.

To cheer him up Vincent brought out the chessboard and the scientist brightened and put the pieces in place. "Watch the pawns," he said. "Poor players always neglect them. But the real power in chess lies with the little pawns, who, though limited in their movements, can, by co-operation, threaten knights, bishops, queens and even kings. There is room for a thesis on the possibility that the game of chess, the most ancient game in the world, provided men with the key to the evolution of democratic forms of government." He went on with his explanation of the game as an exercise in both strategy and philosophy, and Vincent became completely absorbed in it.

Meanwhile there was a tremendous flurry of activity in both the United States and Russia as these two nations readied the most powerful of their rockets to race Grand Fenwick's ambling space ship to the moon—in the guise, of course, of being ready to help the Grand Fenwick astronauts. The United States' effort characteristically started off with a committee meeting of top rocket men, which was unfortunate. These, confronted with the problem of how to get a rocket to the moon and back, split into technical subcommittees to deal with such matters as fuel, air conditioning, interior heat control, exterior heat control, telemetry, waste disposal, health maintenance and psychological aspects of space travel. There was even a librarians' committee to advise on what books should be carried and inside of two days as many as fifteen hundred people were swarming around on the U.S. rocket venture, each convinced that his own aspect of the problem was the one of vital importance.

In vain the President consulted with Dr. Meidel urging him to hasten the American effort and demanding that all red tape be cut and the rocket released. Dr. Meidel had a mind like a mosaic in that, if one tiny stone was missing, this seemed to him more important than the whole picture. He swamped the President with such a deluge of information on the various aspects of the rocket preparation that the Chief Executive was all but drowned in the details and, though he several times lost his temper, was unable to spur the rocket men under Dr. Meidel any faster.

"Even when all is got together," said Dr. Meidel at one of his many meetings with the President, "we still have to take the weather into consideration. And over that, I am afraid, we have no control."

"Weather or no weather, I want that rocket off to get to the moon before the Grand Fenwick rocket," snapped the President.

"Mr. President," said Dr. Meidel, "forgive me for reminding you of the other side of this coin. If we fail—if the rocket explodes, or goes into an orbit in space or crashes on the moon through failure of the landing gear—the disaster would be far more terrible than Grand Fenwick getting there before us. Besides, since the Grand Fenwick rocket is not in communication with the earth, we do not know whether those aboard it are alive. We know that the rocket is still on its way. We are able to pick up the reactor emission on radar. But whether Vincent of Mountjoy and Dr. Kokintz are still alive—that we cannot say."

"All I am asking," said the President, "is that you cut out some of these committee meetings and get the rocket ready."

"Mr. President," said Dr. Meidel smoothly, "you are over-concerned. The U.S. rocket will have a speed of eighty thousand miles an hour. Less than three hours after taking off from Cape Canaveral, it will have reached the moon. We can launch then when the Grand Fenwick rocket is only three thousand miles from the moon, and still get there before them. It is perhaps fortunate," he added, "that they are not in radio communication with earth. Otherwise they might speed up."

With that the President had to be satisfied and the committee meetings of the American "crash program" went on.

In Russia matters were somewhat different. Such committee meetings as were held were convened not for exploration and discussion but so that those involved could report on progress and receive orders. But Russia had her problems too. The only Soviet rocket capable of the journey had been equipped with a space platform in the nose section which had been intended to be put in orbit around the moon. This had to be removed and replaced with a compartment for the two Russian astronauts. This called for a considerable revamping of the Russian rocket and, the Soviet program being rigid, the revamping was difficult to achieve. But the Soviet rocket scientists, like those in America, were confident of success. Their rocket would do 100,000 miles an hour and, being 20,000 miles an hour faster than the American rocket, could readily pass the U.S. space ship even if both were launched at the same time.

The Soviet strategy indeed was to wait for word of the American launching. They would then launch half an hour later, calling world attention to this fact, and when they got to the moon first, would gain all the greater prestige from their late start.

Meanwhile, all in Grand Fenwick were in deep distress about the radio silence from the Duchy's space ship. Tully Bascomb sent signals on his transmitter every hour on the hour but without obtaining contact. The whole Duchy was afraid of what might have happened to their two astronauts, and their fear was such that, by tacit agreement, they did not discuss the radio silence and what it might mean with each other lest in some way the discussion itself might bring about that which they feared.

Gloriana, on the advice of her consort Tully, did issue a short statement to the people of Grand Fenwick on the subject.

"Radio silence from the rocket," the statement said, "cannot but cause us concern. But in every great venture there must be setbacks and we would be unworthy of our two astronauts if we allowed ourselves to become despondent at this point. The rocket is maintaining both its course and its speed, and there can be no question but that both Dr. Kokintz and Vincent of Mountjoy are alive and well. We, whose task it is to wait, must match their courage with our own. In the silences of space, they also must endure this lack of communication which weighs so anxiously upon us. There is here a bond of suffering which, met with patience, will add to the nobility of that which they have set out to achieve. Let us then continue with our daily work in good heart and with trust in God, Who has ever had us in His care."

In a short taped radio interview, Cynthia Bentner said, "I can only pray that all is well and my man will come back safely to me."

The world, divided on every other point, joined in that prayer.

It was not until the fourth day out that the moon began to show any dramatic increase in size to the two astronauts in the Grand Fenwick space ship. On leaving earth's magnifying atmosphere the satellite had been enormously reduced and its growth in the days that followed, though perceptible, was not striking. But on the fourth day it started to swell tremendously and the various "seas" and craters and mountain ranges on it could be plainly seen with the naked eye, though still quite tiny. At the start of the voyage the moon had been at an angle of over fifty degrees from the course of the rocket. That angle, as the moon sped through the heavens at a rate which Dr. Kokintz said was .063 miles per second, to the point at which they would rendezvous with it, had now been reduced to around twenty degrees.

The moon then lay to the right and ahead of the rocket rather than to the right and behind it as had been the case at the start. It was soon the dominant body of the sky, far more imposing than the flaming ball of the sun and the remoter stars. It began now to grow bigger and more majestic with the passing of each hour. Stars, which had been plainly in view before, were lost behind its looming bulk. Craters which, when first seen, had been but the size of match heads, now grew, as the days went by, to the size of shillings and then half-crowns. Vincent was amazed at the extent of them.

"My God!" he cried, examining one huge crater, as big as a football though still sixty or seventy thousand miles off. "How big are those things?"

"That one," said Dr. Kokintz, "is called the Bailly Crater after the man who identified it. It is one hundred and eighty miles in diameter. If we were to land in the center of it, we would not know we were there, for the crater walls would be far out of view over the lunar horizon from us."

"How high are the walls of the craters?" Vincent asked.

"The highest about thirty thousand feet," replied Kokintz. "The equivalent almost of the peak of Mount Everest on Earth. Others are twenty thousand. That would be an average height."

"Steep?" asked Vincent.

"Yes," said Kokintz. "But that won't bother us exploring. Even I, weighing only one-sixth as much as I do on earth, but with the same muscles, will be able to jump fifteen or twenty feet straight up at a leap, on the moon."

Vincent did a little mental arithmetic and said, "In that case we should be able to get to the top of a thirty thousand-foot crater on the moon in an hour."

"Yes," said Kokintz. "Exploring will not be very exhausting. The dangers are from heat, cold, ultraviolet rays and the nature of the surface."

Vincent spent the next several hours rechecking the pressurized space suits obtained (secondhand through war surplus) from the United States along with the rocket. He checked the valves and regulators on the oxygen tanks they would carry on their backs, rather like scuba divers on earth with the difference that they would use re-breathing equipment which would conserve their oxygen while getting rid of carbon dioxide produced in respiration. He was tired when he went to bed and Dr. Kokintz was already asleep, his thick glasses still on his nose. Vincent removed them gently and pulled the metal shutters over the ports of the compartment to produce darkness, for since they were in space and not rotating, there was no day and night on the rocket. It was bathed at all times in the eternal burning merciless light of the sun. The darkness gave him a sense of security but lying on his bunk there came to him for the first time, just before he fell asleep, the sudden acute realization that they were alone in space, dizzily out in the void, far, far from the safety of earth.

He wanted to wake up Dr. Kokintz for comfort, but he didn't. He closed his eyes and forced himself to think of the courtyard of the Castle of Grand Fenwick where he had last seen Cynthia Bentner. The weathered courtyard seemed like a paradise to him now.

XV

When the rocket was a little more than seven days on its journey, it entered the gravitational field of the moon. The effect of the gravity produced a slight acceleration of the rocket's speed. In relation to the surface of the moon, which now loomed before them as a tremendous glittering pockmarked stone ball, the two men in the rocket were now standing upside down, prevented from falling to the ceiling of their compartment by their magnetized boots, which anchored them to the floor. Dr. Kokintz was annoyed, however, to have his glasses slip off his nose and fall to the ceiling, and other objects which were not fastened down floated gently to the ceiling in the same manner, so dreamily, that the two were able to grab them in midair as they drifted off like feathers.

There was nothing in this that was not expected, and Vincent wanted to make a circuit of the moon if possible, photographing that side of it which is always hidden from the world. Kokintz voted against this.

"No tricks," he said. "We must get down as fast as we can, get a few samples of the composition of the surface and then take off again. We are not equipped for sightseeing."

"But it would only take a few hours to make a circuit," said Vincent. "We have plenty of Pinotium and it would be a pity not to do it while we have the chance."

"You are forgetting about the temperatures," said Kokintz. "On the sunless side, the cold will be perhaps a hundred degrees below zero on the Centigrade scale. To suddenly plunge from the terrible heat into that cold would cause the whole rocket to contract so fast that it might crumble into pieces. We will go ahead with our plan, which was to land in the twilight zone on the moon where we can hope the temperatures will not be extreme. That is the safest place for us. And since the lunar day lasts about thirty of our days on earth, the twilight zone will persist for a long time to protect us. I repeat—no tricks. Remember that we are in a place we are not designed to be in."

Vincent agreed, though with some reluctance; and with the lunar surface but six thousand miles or six hours' travel distant, so that it filled the whole sky before them, turned to the task of preparing the rocket for its landing.

At Cape Canaveral all was ready for the launching of the six-stage U.S. space ship to the moon, and Dr. Meidel, with six hours in which to reach it with the rocket, was feeling very pleased with himself. The two American astronauts, fully dressed for space travel, were in the ready room with Dr. Meidel and the President, who had come to Cape Canaveral for the launching.

"We have plenty of time in hand, Mr. President," said Dr. Meidel. "We will launch in two hours' time and get to the moon an hour before Grand Fenwick. Everything has been checked and rechecked and the weather reports are favorable. I am sure you will agree that this method—the scientific approach—is the best after all."

The President nodded. He was highly nervous and excited and hardly heard what Dr. Meidel was saying.

"When will the fueling be done?" he asked. He knew the answer for he had a timetable of the whole of the last-minute procedure before him. But he felt the need to ask a question, just to relieve his anxiety.

"In one hour," replied Meidel, looking at the clock in the ready room. "It is in its final stages."

The President turned to the two astronauts. "I won't feel happy until you boys are successfully on your way," he said.

"Nor we either," said one of them with a grin.

There was a battery of telephones on a table in the ready room and one of these started ringing now. All four present gave a little start and stared at it, and Dr. Meidel picked the instrument up.

"Meidel, ready room," he said into the mouthpiece and then listened for what seemed to be an age.

"Bring it in to me immediately," he said and put down the receiver and looked at the President, his face ashen.

"What is it?" asked the President.

Before Dr. Meidel could answer a man clad in flame-proof coveralls came into the room and, ignoring the President, put a sheet of tissue paper on the table.

"We found it in the filtering system," he said.

They all stared at the piece of paper. In the center of it lay a little black blob.

"What is it?" demanded the President testily.

"A fly, sir," said the man in the coveralls.

"A fly?" echoed the President.

"Yes, sir," said the man. "It was in the kerosene. The fuel, for the rocket."

"Well, what of it?" demanded the President. "It was filtered out. That's what the filters are for, I presume."

"Only half the fly in here, Mr. President," said Dr. Meidel.

"It is reasonable to assume that the other half somehow got into the rocket. We will have to unbunker the rocket and refilter all the kerosene." He glanced at the clock. "That means we can't make it first to the moon, I'm afraid," he said. "It will take four hours to unload and refuel."

"Damnation!" cried the President. "For half a fly! We are to be beaten to the moon for half a fly? Do you mean to tell me that half a fly that may or may not be in the fuel tanks of that rocket, means that we are to be beaten to the moon?"

"I'm afraid so, Mr. President," said Dr. Meidel. "We can't risk the whole rocket and the lives of these two men when there is a reasonable certainty of impurities in the fuel. Of course, if you give the order, we will go ahead. But my advice is to empty the bunkers and refilter all the kerosene."

The President glanced at the two astronauts. They said nothing but seemed to be pleading with him to give the order to go ahead anyway. He looked from them to the mutilated corpse of the fly and then said inaudibly, "All right. Refuel." Then he got up and left the ready room.

In Russia the Soviet scientists waited patiently for news of the American take-off. The launching site was in a remote area, far to the east of the Urals, and a radio signal from Moscow was needed to give the word for the blast-off. The Russian astronauts were already in their capsule and the rocket fully fueled. But the hours went by and no signal came and the rocket remained on the launching pad.

The Grand Fenwick rocket landed on the moon without any incident whatever. By changing the angle of thrust of the shower nozzles which he was using for jets, Vincent was able to turn the rocket on its side so that it was parallel to the moon and then upended it to land it gently in the center of a large lunar crater on the extensible legs, which were operated electrically. The touchdown was so soft that there was not the slightest jar. He cut off the reactor and the two looked in silence at each other.

"Well, we made it," said Vincent at length.

"Certainly we made it," said Dr. Kokintz. "The matter was never in any doubt. Now let us get outside and get our samples and then take off again."

"We ought to explore a little," said Vincent. "We could spend a day and then come back to the rocket. In a day we could cover a lot of territory. Besides, we have to put up the flag."

"What flag?" asked Dr. Kokintz, struggling into his space suit.

"A Grand Fenwick flag," said Vincent. "We have to plant it on the moon to take possession in the name of Grand Fenwick. I promised my father before we left. He prepared a little speech which I have to read and you are to make a tape of it and take a picture of Grand Fenwick's flag floating over the moon."

"It won't float," said Dr. Kokintz. "There's no wind. No atmosphere."

"Well, I'll hold it out and then you'll take the picture."

When they had their space suits on, had checked them for leaks and to see that the pressure was that of the earth's atmosphere at the surface, they both entered a small airlock in the side of the rocket. Kokintz had a camera and a portable battery-operated tape recorder with him, and Vincent carried a flagstaff with, at its head, the double-headed eagle banner of Grand Fenwick saying "Aye" from one beak and "Nay" from the other.

They shut the door of the airlock behind them and then opened the exterior door leading outward to the moon. There was a tremendous hiss as the door opened and the air in it rushed outward into the lunar vacuum. Both were swept off their feet, sailing out of the rocket and landing fifty or more feet from it.

"You hurt, Doctor?" asked Vincent, switching on his walkie-talkie. (There being no atmosphere, communication between the two had to be by radio.)

"No," said the scientist. "It was stupid of me to let you open that door so fast. Well, one can't think of everything on an expedition of this sort." They dusted themselves off and looked around. The prospect before them was of utter bleakness and the starkest solitude. Vincent felt that he had landed on a drawing done in black ink on blinding white paper. Something seemed horribly wrong about the perspective and when he took a step forward he felt dizzy.

"There's something the matter with it," he said. "It looks all wrong."

"It is the lack of atmosphere," said Kokintz. "The mountains in the distance are as sharply outlined as the ones close by. There is no air to soften things as they become distant as there is on earth. The shadows are all jet-black, the highlights blinding white."

"I feel like I'm going to bump into one of those mountain walls next step," Vincent said.

"You'll get used to it," said Kokintz.

"Well, we'd better get the flag raised," said Vincent. He glanced around and, seeing a rocky escarpment only twenty feet away, got to it in two bounds. Kokintz followed, drifting through the air at each step like Peter Pan with a soap bubble over his head. They got to the top of the escarpment without trouble and Vincent produced a sheet of paper in his father's handwriting from a pocket in his space suit.

"Got the tape recorder hooked up to your receiver?" he asked.

"Yes," said Kokintz. He wasn't paying much attention but was looking up at the sky rather anxiously. Vincent started to read from the paper as follows:

"Know all men by these Presents, that I, Vincent of Mountjoy, on behalf of the Duchy of Grand Fenwick, a sovereign and independent nation on the planet known as Earth, do here and now claim complete sovereignty over all the territories of that satellite of Earth known as the Moon on which, together with Dr. Theodore Kokintz, I am the first man to land. In token of our claim to possession of the Moon as a territory of the Duchy of Grand Fenwick to be subject in every way to the laws of the Duchy, I now raise the flag of Grand Fenwick on this peak and call upon all the nations of the Earth to respect the rights here asserted. God Save the Duchess Gloriana XII. May she live forever."

With that Vincent raised the flag, thrusting the staff into the pumice-like stone of the escarpment. He had no sooner done this than he was smothered in a shower of tin cans which floated down out of the heavens about him, as if the earth, having listened to his speech, had thrown all its garbage at him. Empty cans of barbecued beans, of frankfurters, sauerkraut, condensed milk, beer, Coca-Cola, together with glass jars that had once contained peanut butter, pickled herrings and grape jelly—in fact, all the garbage which he had thrust out of the rocket during their nine-day journey from earth, now clattered around in a pile which buried both him and the flag.

"Damnation!" roared Vincent, fighting his way out of this pile. "Who did that?"

"You did," said Kokintz. "That's all the garbage you threw out of the rocket." He surveyed the odious pile sadly. "Even without a flag," he said, "it would be plain that people from earth were here."

Vincent started to move the cans and bottles aside. He found that he could kick an empty can a good quarter of a mile. But Dr. Kokintz was upset. "Such a litter," he said. "It would be better to dig a hole and bury them. What a disgrace—to come all this way and make the moon into a garbage dump."

He was so distressed that Vincent helped dig a hole and bury the cans and bottles, though this seemed a curious way to spend part of their precious time on the moon. The actual task of digging was not difficult. The moon's surface at this place was composed of material rather like soft pumice stone, covered with a couple of inches of fine powder. Beneath it the rock was cracked and they could lift up huge pieces with their hands. They soon had a hole big enough for the cans and bottles. But when they looked up from their work, they found they were swathed in a fog so heavy that though they could see each other the rocket, not more than a few yards away, had utterly disappeared.

"Pumice dust," said Kokintz. "With the low lunar gravity, it will probably take an hour for it to settle again. Come. We must walk out of it."

He led the way, Vincent following. Two steps took them twelve feet and well out of the column of dust which rose a hundred feet up over the area they had been working. The top of the column, catching the rays of the sun, glittered with an angelic light. Kokintz studied it with interest. Then he turned and bounded across the bottom of the crater to the lip, which he proceeded to climb. Vincent followed him. The lip of the crater was rimmed with sunlight as with liquid fire. There the heat would be appalling, a terrible challenge even in an insulated space suit. To Vincent's surprise, Kokintz bent down, picked up two handfuls of dust and flung them up over the lip of the crater. Immediately a vast smoke screen was laid over the area, casting a soft shadow on the side away from the sun.

"What are you up to?" asked Vincent.

"Investigating a method of exploring the side of the moon exposed to the sun," replied Kokintz. "It is very simple. All that is needed is to make a smoke screen with the dust and walk in the shadow of it."

"Hang the dust," said Vincent. "It gives me the willies. We could lose each other or the rocket in a minute. What causes it, anyway?"

"Alternating heat and cold," said Kokintz. "It has reduced the surface of the moon to powder. The powder acts as an insulator to protect what is below. But it is plain that the moon is gradually crumbling away. Soon it will be nothing but a ball of dust, no more solid than a fog bank."

"How soon?" asked Vincent.

"In about a billion years," said Kokintz.

"Then we can let someone else worry about that," said Vincent. "Come on. Let's look around some more."

But first they decided to try the radio again and call Grand Fenwick to announce that they had landed on the moon and taken possession of it in the name of the Duchy. They returned to the rocket, entering through the airlock, into which they pumped sufficient air to bring the pressure to that of the earth's surface.

"Eagle calling Grand Fenwick," signaled Vincent, that being the code agreed on. "Eagle calling Grand Fenwick."

"Come in, Eagle," said the voice of Tully. "Is that you, Vincent? Are you safe? Is all well? What happened?"

"Everything is fine," said Vincent. "The radio went out but it is working now. We've landed on the moon safely, half an hour ago. What do you want us to do with it?"

"I'm proud of you, my boy. Proud of you," came in the trembling voice of the Count of Mountjoy. "This is indeed a magnificent day in the history of our country. Not even Spain in the great days of Columbus and of Magellan could point to a feat as magnificent as you have achieved on behalf of your native land. Have you seen any sign of the others?"

"What others?" asked Vincent.

"The Russians and the Americans?"

"Are they supposed to be about?" cried Vincent, very surprised.

"They took off two hours ago," said the Count of Mountjoy. "Officially, both nations have sent rockets capable of tremendous velocity to the moon to help you, should you get into any trouble. Actually, it is a face-saving device, and I suspect that there is more to it than that. I suspect that both the Russian and the United States astronauts, on landing, have been instructed to claim the moon for their different countries. You are sure you got there first?"

"Positive," said Vincent. "Absolutely nobody around when we got out of the rocket. That's right, isn't it, Doctor?"

"Yes," said Kokintz. "How are the bobolinks?"

"Hang the bobolinks!" shouted Mountjoy. "Now listen to this very carefully. We are at a time of crisis and the fate of the world for generations to come may be in the balance. It is vital to humanity that our claim to the moon be fully established.

"I am going to announce your arrival on the moon ahead of any other nation and announce that you have claimed the moon for Grand Fenwick. That should take it out of the East-West conflict and will be of immense value to everybody. I expect to be able to rally the support of all the smaller members of the United Nations for our claim—though I am unsure of the Arab bloc. Anyway, if the Americans and Russians arrive and attempt to raise their standards on the moon, you are to demand that they take them down. If they do not comply, you may resort to whatever force is necessary to make them comply."

"We are not here an hour and you want us to start a war?" asked Kokintz.

"Quite the wrong way of looking at it," said the Count of Mountjoy. "I want you to ensure the peace by the threat of war. Militant pacifism. Pacifism alone is nothing short of warmongering. It should be possible to enter into an alliance with the Americans, if this is necessary, by discreet promises of mineral rights, to join you against the Russians. That would make the odds overwhelming—four to two—and ensure your success. Is there anything further you want to know?"

Vincent looked bleakly at Kokintz. "There is one thing I would like to know," said Kokintz.

"What is that?" asked the Count of Mountjoy.

"How are the bobolinks?"

"Damnation!" said the Count of Mountjoy, quite beside himself.

"Fine," said Tully. "I think the eggs will be hatched in two or three days."

"That is the only good news I have heard on the moon, so far," said Kokintz, and that ended the communication.

They got out of the rocket into the terrifying, sharp, perspectiveless landscape of the moon again and headed for the lip of the crater, soaring over the ground like thistledown. Beyond the lip of the crater was a massive and gaunt peak. It rose in the form of a triangle, one side of it a blinding white in the sunlight, the other side the deepest black. By common consent they decided to scale this peak, which would give them a tremendous view over the moon. The peak seemed to be but a mile away, but proved to be some ten miles distant so that they were something like an hour in gaining the base of it, though able to take ten-foot strides over the surface.

They crossed a number of big canyons or fissures which were, in places, fifteen feet wide. Here they stopped on one rim and with a medium jump sailed readily over to the other side. Dr. Kokintz looked very peculiar jumping, for when he was halfway over these canyons, he would, in a burst of scientific enthusiasm, crane his head and trunk down to see into them as much as he could, so that once he performed a slow somersault over a fissure and at another time landed on his back on the other side.

"You've got to be more careful," warned Vincent. "If you rip that space suit, you'll be dead in a moment."

In a little while they had gained the base of the peak, which was of some sixteen thousand feet. They rested a little, looking back over the trail they had come, which was plainly marked by a kind of intermittent smoke screen of dust raised during their progress and not yet settled back to the ground. Then they climbed to the summit without much more labor than a man might experience in going up a flight of stairs on earth. When they got to the top they found on the other side an even bigger crater than the one in which they had landed. Dr. Kokintz estimated the distance across it as eighty miles. Beyond that was a range of mountains, small, to be sure, because of the distance, but plainly seen, the edges as sharp as the teeth of a saw. Some of these mountains were very high so that the horizon, which was ringed with them, was like a fringe of pyramids against the jet-black sky in which the sun blazed, a huge glowing ball which it was impossible to look at directly. As they stood looking toward this appalling horizon which, though so distant, seemed near enough to touch, earth raised herself over the lunar desolation—a lovely huge blue liquid jewel, hung in a sky of sable. The sight was so entrancing that neither of them could speak. It was magnificent beyond anything they had ever seen, and the light which earth now gave to the moon was not the harsh, blinding light of the burning sun, but a gentle bluish light, consoling as a benediction, taking the savagery out of the terrible craters and fissures and mountains of the moon and investing them with a softness that made them almost lovely in turn.

"I never knew it was so beautiful," said Vincent at last. "It is lovely beyond everything else in all the heavens."

"It is our home," said Dr. Kokintz simply and sadly.

XVI

The splendid light which the earth threw on the moon was much stronger than the brightest moonlight experienced on earth and Kokintz and Vincent, a couple of little dots on the top of a gaunt peak, with bubbles for heads, spent a long time just watching the earth soaring up into the black heavens. The stars seen from the moon were very much brighter than from earth, and there were literally millions more of them. There were so many of them, in fact, that the familiar constellations of the earth's sky—the Big Dipper, the belt of Orion, the sword of Orion, and the twin stars, Castor and Pollux were hardly to be found in the profusion. Vincent was quite lost as far as placing the points of the compass was concerned. No earth compass would work on the moon, and unable to find the Big Dipper he could not place the celestial north. But Dr. Kokintz, with a glance at the rising earth and the last fiery tip of the setting sun, named the cardinal points for him, explaining, however, that these were the points as known on earth.

"There's no north in space," he said. "It's just a name we use on earth for our convenience. But if it will comfort you, north is that way and the rocket, over there, is to the south-southeast." Vincent turned around to look at the rocket.

"Look," he shouted. "A tiny shooting star. Over there. . . . By golly, there's two of them." He pointed excitedly to the southern horizon where two points of light, hardly of the magnitude of pinpricks in the diamond blaze of the heavens, were flashing against the sable sky. It was hard to follow them. They were lost as soon as they got in the neighborhood of any of the glittering stars and, the stars being present in such multitudes, only occasional and fleeting glimpses of the moving pinpoints could be caught.

"Russia and the United States," said Dr. Kokintz. "It looks like a dead heat."

It was a dead heat. The two rockets zoomed toward the moon, hardly increasing in size for quite a few seconds, and then suddenly becoming very big and flashing even brighter than the stars, for they were high enough above the moon's surface to catch the rays of the sun. They were nose to nose as they plummeted down. They zoomed over the peak on which Kokintz and Vincent were sitting, noiseless as ghosts; and then, as if both were controlled by the same hand, they upended themselves and settled down in the huge crater at the foot of the peak, with all the precision of a couple of ballet dancers. They landed perhaps two miles from the peak, but could be as plainly seen as if they were but a few yards away.

No sooner were the rockets firmly settled on their extensible legs than doors opened, and out of each of the rockets jumped two men in bubble-headed space suits. They exchanged hurried glances, looked anxiously around, and both pairs made for a small eminence near the rockets. They got there in the same second and one man in each pair erected a long pole firmly on the eminence while the other two backed off apparently to take photographs.

Vincent glanced at Kokintz. Kokintz was looking up in the sky.

Then it happened. Two separate showers of tin cans and bottles rained down on the two astronauts who had but a moment before raised their standards to claim the moon for their respective nations.

"There is a lot more to be said for garbage than I had

thought," said Dr. Kokintz mildly. "Come, let us go and meet our enemies."

When they got to the little eminence a few minutes later, a heavy argument was raging between the two Russian astronauts and the two American astronauts. It was conducted in English and Vincent and Kokintz could hear it over their own radios.

"Take that thing down," said the American astronaut. "This is American territory."

"I have claimed the moon for the Union of Soviet Socialist Republics and the workers of the world," said the Russian astronaut.

"What you need is a punch in the nose," said the American.

"I will not bow down before imperialist hyenas and aggressors," said the Russian.

"Welcome to the moon," said Dr. Kokintz, cutting in.

The four whirled around to look at Kokintz and Vincent. "Where did you come from?" demanded one of the Russians.

"The Duchy of Grand Fenwick," said Vincent. "By the way, you people are now on the territory of the Duchy of Grand Fenwick. Do any of you have a visa?"

"What the hell do you mean, visas?" demanded one of the Americans.

"It's very simple," said Vincent calmly. "We got here first—a clear hour ahead of you. We have claimed the moon for the Duchy of Grand Fenwick. A visa is required by any alien entering the territory of the Duchy of Grand Fenwick. So I repeat. Have any of you got visas?"

All four of them looked blankly at Vincent and then at each other.

"I see that you haven't," said Vincent. "Well, we are interested in encouraging the tourist trade, so I don't want to appear discourteous to you. The circumstances are, I will admit, unusual. If all four of you will step over to the Grand Fenwick rocket, I will give you permits to land. The fee is one pound sterling but you can pay that when you get back to earth. However, I must insist that you take down those flags."

"I will never take down the glorious banner of the comrade workers of the Union of Soviet Socialist Republics," said one of the Russians.

"I'm not going to make a speech about it," said one of the Americans, "but we are not going to haul down Old Glory for you."

"In that case," said Vincent, "you are both committing an open act of aggression against the Duchy of Grand Fenwick, an act of aggression, I might add, which is quite unprovoked. I will report this immediately to the Duchy by microwave and the matter will be taken up before the United Nations in a few hours. I think you ought to consider what you are doing. Do both of you want to appear before the world as contriving to get to the moon merely to commit an unprovoked act of aggression against the smallest nation on earth?"

Again there was an exchange of glances but no move to lower the banners.

"I will give you an hour to think it over," said Vincent. "You will perhaps want to consult with your governments. I think you ought to know that the news of our prior arrival here and our taking possession of the moon in the name of Grand Fenwick has already been radioed back to earth and broadcast all over the world. It is hardly possible then for either of you to pretend to be the first arrivals. Our rocket is over the ridge there and I will expect to see you there at the end of an hour. If you do not appear, I will reluctantly have to report to my government that an act of aggression has been committed against us by your governments, and the matter will be immediately placed before the United Nations."

Still they stared at him, not saying a word.

"It will look rather peculiar," continued Vincent smoothly, "if the world learns that, having come here on the pretext of standing by to help us in case of trouble, you instead indulged in what can only be called a vulgar piece of claim-jumping. Come on, Doctor."

He led the doctor away and the two took up a position on a nearby ridge to watch what happened.

The first thing that happened was a consultation between the two Russian astronauts. Although the words could be plainly heard by all present, they were unintelligible, for the Russians were speaking in their own language. They then returned to their rocket but immediately reappeared armed with spades and crowbars.

"What do you suppose they are going to do now?" asked Vincent.

"I think they are going to build a wall," said Dr. Kokintz.

It was true. The two Russians started flinging up lumps of pumice and other rocks into a wall which, work being ridiculously easy on the moon, soon extended for two hundred yards and was six feet high—as closely as could be seen through the dust. The American astronauts had gone into their rocket presumably to consult with their government and returned to see the wall dividing their rocket from the Russian rocket. They looked at each other dumbfounded, and then one of them, without a word, took a prodigious leap. He soared twenty feet up in the air, cleared the wall like a bird and came down gently on the other side.

"Seems that walls don't work on the moon," said Vincent. "Come on. Let's go back to the rocket. Wish we had something more to eat than the pickled herring and those darned barbecued Western-style baked beans."

They were hardly back at the rocket, however, before both the Americans and Russians appeared at the entry port.

"We've taken down our flag after consulting with Washington," said one of the Americans. "The moon is yours."

"We've taken down our flag in the interest of co-existence and peace among the workers of the world," said one of the Russians. "The moon is yours—for the present."

"Excellent," said Vincent. "Come on in and I'll give you your landing permits and make it all legal. By the way, do any of you fellows have anything on board other than Western-style barbecued baked beans? We're a little overstocked with them."

XVII

Two hours later the Grand Fenwick rocket took off for earth, but since it poked back through space at a mere thousand miles an hour, it arrived several days after the return of both the Russian and the American rockets, which rather took the edge off the homecoming.

To be sure, the return to Grand Fenwick, where the rocket landed neatly in the courtyard of the castle, produced a tumultuous welcome. The band turned out playing a choice selection of martial tunes, the castle was decorated with pennons and bannerets, the children had their faces thoroughly scrubbed for the occasion and were all in their best Sunday clothes, and Gloriana XII presented Dr. Kokintz and Vincent of Mountjoy with a medal struck especially for the occasion. On one side was an engraving of the rocket taking off for the moon while on the other was an excellent reproduction of an American shower head (this, at the insistence of the Count of Mountjoy) with beneath it the well-known Latin tag "Per ardua ad astra."

Cynthia Bentner could hardly say a word when Vincent got out of the rocket but ran to embrace him and kissed him as soon as he got the bubble helmet off his head. She then immediately demanded that he put it back again lest he catch a cold. A big banquet was held that night, preceded by a tour of the twenty elaborate bathrooms with which the castle had been fitted.

Still, the world effect of the return of Grand Fenwick's rocket was less than a sensation. Press and radio coverage was good, but not astounding. After all, the world press and radio and television had welcomed two rockets from the moon back to earth already and the return of the Grand Fenwick rocket began to border on repetition. This rather annoyed the Count of Mountjoy, who felt that Grand Fenwick had been robbed of its rightful prominence. After the banquet, he took his son Vincent aside and said:

"You did splendidly, my boy, in raising our banner on the moon before the others and so claiming it for Grand Fenwick. Not that we have any real use for it. I propose, subject to the approval of the Council of Freemen, of course, to turn the moon over to the United Nations as being the proper body to administer the planets. Our claim is quite firm, I think. We were there first and raised our flag first and the whole world was informed that we had arrived before the others. That is quite clear. It is a pity, however, that there is nothing in writing acknowledging our sovereignty. A great pity. The Americans can be relied upon to honor their commitments. But the Russians trouble me. They are great sticklers for the written word, you know. If it is not in writing, it isn't legal as far as they are concerned."

Vincent fumbled in his pocket, took out his wallet and from it extracted two pieces of paper.

"We have something in writing," he said. "Here it is," He handed the two pieces of paper to his father. They were copies of the landing permits he had issued to the American and Russian astronauts.

One read:

I, Vincent of Mountjoy, on behalf of the government of the Duchy of Grand Fenwick, do hereby grant permission to the two American astronauts, Colonel Charles Seibert and Colonel Wilbur Reeves, to land on the moon, which is part of the territory of the Duchy of Grand Fenwick, on payment of one pound sterling. The aforementioned, having no currency of the Duchy with them, are hereby authorized to pay the fee for this landing permit in kind by providing two chickens and one canned ham to myself as representative of the Duchy, receipt of which is hereby acknowledged.

Signed: Vincent of Mountjoy.

The second piece of paper, issued to the Russian astronauts, was identical except that the landing fee was two one-kilogram cans of borscht and a blood sausage weighing one kilogram. Both papers bore not only the signature of Vincent of Mountjoy but also the signatures of the astronauts to whom they had been issued.

"Excellent, my boy!" cried the Count of Mountjoy. "Excellent. By Jove, I see the makings of a great statesman in you yet. Engineering is all very well for people of a certain intelligence, but the full scope of man in all his vigor, his cunning and his imaginative powers, is reserved for statesmanship. You will be a great prime minister of the Duchy of Grand Fenwick one of these days. Make no mistake about it."

"I thought it better to get some written acknowledgment of our claim to the moon from our two principal rivals," said Vincent. "But I must confess that I little thought that the moon was to be had for two chickens, one canned ham, some borscht and a blood sausage."

"Ummmmm," said the Count of Mountjoy thoughtfully, "the incident is not quite without precedent. The whole of Manhattan Island was obtained, I fancy, for rather less."

Later that night, the Count of Mountjoy luxuriated in his huge bathtub of polished pale-green Connemara marble and thought how splendidly everything had come out. The hot water was magnificent, and available in the most generous quantities. Running hot and cold water was now featured in all the homes in Grand Fenwick. A wing of the castle had been fitted up for the start of what he knew would be a most profitable tourist trade—though Bentner would fight that tooth and nail. The moon was to be internationalized. And it was all, so he reasoned, the fruit of his own work.

Of course, every penny of the American money had been spent. Every penny. But it had been worth it. And there was really nothing more that required to be bought—nothing at all.

Suddenly he sat bolt upright in his bath.

"Oh, my God!" he exclaimed. "The fur coat. We forgot the Imperial Russian Sable fur coat for Her Grace the Duchess!"

The United States Secretary of State surveyed the stack of Red Folders on his desk and saw on top of the pile a folder with which he had become all too familiar in recent weeks. He reached for it with a sinking heart, opened it and there found a letter on the elaborate stationery of the Duchy of

Grand Fenwick. Like a man in a trance he started to read the letter. It went:

The Secretary of State,
Government of the United States of America,
Washington, D.C.

Greetings:

I have the honor, as the Principal Minister of State of the Duchess Gloriana XII, to apply for a loan of $50,000 for the purpose of purchasing a fur coat for Her Grace the Duchess to surprise her on her birthday. . . .

"Oh no!" groaned the Secretary of State. "No! Not again!"

He stared at the letter for a moment in horror and disbelief and was about to call for his expert on Central European affairs, Frederick Paxton Wendover, but changed his mind. Instead he reached for the telephone and said into the mouthpiece, "Give me Saks Fifth Avenue, New York City." The connection was made in a moment and the Secretary of State asked for the fur department.

"This is the Secretary of State," he said, "and I might add this is an emergency. I want you to send to the Duchess Gloriana XII of Grand Fenwick immediately one Imperial Russian Sable fur coat, full length, and send the bill to me personally at the State Department. It is for my private account. There's only one thing. I don't know her size."

"That would be size twelve, Mr. Secretary," said the man at Saks Fifth Avenue.

"How do you know?" asked the Secretary, surprised.

"We make it our business to know the size of everyone in the world of sufficient eminence to one day buy an Imperial Russian Sable fur coat," was the reply.

"Well, I'll be damned," said the Secretary and he hung up.

Gloriana loved the fur coat and in an address of gratitude to the Council of Freemen said that no sovereign in the world was better served than she.

As for the bobolinks, they hatched out a thriving family of four which, when they had grown sufficiently, took off on the annual migration to the South American continent, but did not return the following year to Grand Fenwick.

"They had their little adventure," said Kokintz philosophically to Tully. "For them it was quite as big a journey as our trip to the moon. They are not likely to repeat it."

"About Pinotium Sixty-four . . . ," said Tully.

"Ah yes," said Kokintz. "A pity it only occurs in a Premier

Grand Cru Grand Fenwick wine. And nobody can say when a Premier Grand Cru crop will occur. It is, like everything else, in the hands of God."

"Yes," said Tully soberly. "In the hands of God."